WRONG FO

"It's got to be h
here while Sean
having fun," Mitch

"It's not so bad. And knowing you has made the hospital much more bearable." Impulsively, I kissed him gently on the cheek. Without a word, he kissed me back, this time on the lips. It felt warm and soft and gentle, all the things a kiss should be. As we broke apart, I looked up and was shocked to see Sean's steely hazel eyes looking down at me.

"Uh, hi, there," I said with a gulp. Turning away from Mitch, I went on, "Nice to see you, Sean."

"Is it?" he asked.

"I can see I'd better be going," Mitch said. He stood up and extended his hand to Sean. "Nice to meet you. I've heard lots of good things about you from Gretchen. You've got a fine girlfriend, Sean. Take good care of her."

Sean didn't take his hand. He didn't say anything. He just stood there, watching Mitch head toward the door.

Bantam Sweet Dreams Romances
Ask your bookseller for the books you have missed

1 P.S. I LOVE YOU
2 THE POPULARITY PLAN
3 LAURIE'S SONG
5 LITTLE SISTER
6 CALIFORNIA GIRL
8 THE THOROUGHBRED
9 COVER GIRL
10 LOVE MATCH
12 NIGHT OF THE PROM
13 THE SUMMER JENNY FELL IN LOVE
14 DANCE OF LOVE
18 TEN-BOY SUMMER
20 THE POPULARITY SUMMER
22 SECRET IDENTITY
23 FALLING IN LOVE AGAIN
24 THE TROUBLE WITH CHARLIE
26 IT MUST BE MAGIC
30 LITTLE WHITE LIES
32 DAYDREAMER
35 FORBIDDEN LOVE
36 SUMMER DREAMS
39 FIRST LOVE
41 THE TRUTH ABOUT ME & BOBBY V.
45 DREAM PROM
50 LIGHTS, CAMERA, LOVE
53 GHOST OF A CHANCE
54 I CAN'T FORGET YOU
55 SPOTLIGHT ON LOVE
56 CAMPFIRE NIGHTS
57 ON HER OWN
58 RHYTHM OF LOVE
59 PLEASE SAY YES
60 SUMMER BREEZES
61 EXCHANGE OF HEARTS
62 JUST LIKE THE MOVIES
63 KISS ME, CREEP
64 LOVE IN THE FAST LANE
65 THE TWO OF US
66 LOVE TIMES TWO
67 I BELIEVE IN YOU
68 LOVEBIRDS
69 CALL ME BEAUTIFUL
70 SPECIAL SOMEONE
71 TOO MANY BOYS
72 GOODBYE FOREVER
73 LANGUAGE OF LOVE
74 DON'T FORGET ME
75 FIRST SUMMER LOVE
76 THREE CHEERS FOR LOVE
77 TEN-SPEED SUMMER
78 NEVER SAY NO
79 STAR STRUCK!
80 A SHOT AT LOVE
81 SECRET ADMIRER
82 HEY, GOOD LOOKING!
83 LOVE BY THE BOOK
84 THE LAST WORD
85 THE BOY SHE LEFT BEHIND
86 QUESTIONS OF LOVE
87 PROGRAMMED FOR LOVE
88 WRONG KIND OF BOY
89 101 WAYS TO MEET MR. RIGHT
90 TWO'S A CROWD
91 THE LOVE HUNT
92 KISS AND TELL
93 THE GREAT BOY CHASE
94 SECOND CHANCES
95 NO STRINGS ATTACHED
96 FIRST, LAST, AND ALWAYS
97 DANCING IN THE DARK
98 LOVE IS IN THE AIR
99 ONE BOY TOO MANY
100 FOLLOW THAT BOY
101 WRONG FOR EACH OTHER
102 HEARTS DON'T LIE

Wrong For Each Other

Debra Spector

BANTAM BOOKS
TORONTO • NEW YORK • LONDON • SYDNEY • AUCKLAND

RL 6, IL age 11 and up

WRONG FOR EACH OTHER
A Bantam Book / February 1986

Cover photo by Pat Hill

ISBN 0-553-25366-2

Published simultaneously in the United States and Canada

Bantam Books are published by Bantam Books, Inc. Its trademark, consisting of the words "Bantam Books" and the portrayal of a rooster, is registered in U.S. Patent and Trademark Office and in other countries. Marca Registrada. Bantam Books, Inc., 666 Fifth Avenue, New York, New York 10103.

Printed and bound in Great Britain by Hunt Barnard Printing Ltd.

O 0 9 8 7 6 5 4 3 2 1

To Straw

Chapter One

I'd been excited about it ever since I'd heard that my friend Lindsay Tompkins was having a Sweet Sixteen birthday party. It promised to be one big event, with a live band, catered food, the works. Everyone around Brimley High had been talking about the party ever since Lindsay had sent out the blue engraved invitations a few weeks earlier. My friends and I usually had smaller, more informal parties, so everyone was anticipating something really special at Lindsay's bash.

I had just finished getting ready for the party when I heard the door bell ring. I took one last look in the mirror, then hurried downstairs to meet my boyfriend Sean. I said a quick goodbye to my mom, then Sean and I hurried down the flagstone steps that led to the street.

Sean Flanders, all six feet, two and a half

inches of him, stopped before opening the passenger side door to give me a quick hug. "You look great, Gretchen," he said, casting an admiring glance at my dress.

"Thank you, Sean." I wanted to look just right for him and had spent all day experimenting with makeup and different styles for my shoulder-length dark brown hair.

I suppose I was being silly. Sean certainly wasn't the first boy I'd ever dated, but going out with him had been a dream come true. And I never wanted him to think I was taking him for granted.

My best friend Melinda, who happened to be Sean's twin sister, and I had talked for hours before the party about what we were going to wear. I'd finally bought a flame red sateen dress with puffed sleeves. I'd accented it with deep red nail polish, a silver belt, and textured red tights. As a finishing touch, I added oversize black lacquer earrings and a string of black beads. Red is an unusual color for me; I usually prefer more subtle colors such as lavender, rose, or aqua. But Melinda had commented on how well the bright color complimented my blue eyes.

Sean turned to me. "So, what do you think?"

"You look terrific, too," I said. "But then you

always do." Terrific was definitely an understatement. With dark hazel eyes and blond hair the color of sun-dried straw, Sean was every Brimley girl's dream. That night he wore pleated gray pants, a pale blue shirt, and an ice blue and gray plaid sweater that made him look as if he'd be at home in any men's fashion magazine.

"Not me, silly," he said, laughing. "I meant Baby."

Baby was the name Melinda had given to Sean's car, a silver Trans Am. Sean had bought it several months earlier, spending every penny of the money he'd been putting away since he was ten. The car wasn't new, but Sean had put so much work into it that it looked as if it were. He'd installed a new stereo and new sheepskin seat covers, and he washed it every day.

"I just rewaxed her this afternoon."

"Looks great," I said. It was dark outside, but I could still see the street lamp reflected perfectly on the front hood. "You going to let me drive tonight?"

"Not on your life," he said seriously.

"I guess I'll live," I countered, joining in the joke.

I knew Sean would sooner sell his soul than let anyone else sit behind the steering wheel.

And truthfully, I didn't mind. I didn't think I could handle such a high-powered car, but I loved teasing him about letting me try.

I still found it hard to believe we were dating. I'd known Sean for ages, but it wasn't until that year that our friendship became something more. We shared a study period, and one day he passed me a note. The note asked if I knew there were fifty-eight slats on the white miniblinds that hung over the windows. I smiled back at him, and the rest, you might say, was history. At the time I jokingly told Melinda that Sean only started going out with me because he'd already dated every other girl at Brimley. She'd wasted no time in setting me straight.

"He's crazy about you," she'd told me. "I don't think he can believe he's missed what's been right under his nose all this time."

I was stirred from my thoughts when I heard Sean asking, "All set?" He opened the door and motioned for me to get in.

"I can't wait," I said, anticipating a night of fun—and romance.

Lindsay lived a few miles away in a fabulous house high on a hill overlooking Brimley, a town just outside Los Angeles. I leaned back in my seat, enjoying the feel of the breeze coming in through the open sunroof. Usually it was too chilly to open it in January, but that night was unusually warm and clear. The weather was perfect for what I knew was going to be a perfect night.

Sean took my hand in his. "What time do you have to be back tonight?"

"One o'clock."

"What do you say we leave the party a little before one and stop off at the bluff off Wonderland Skyway? It looks as though there'll be plenty of stars out tonight."

"Sounds wonderful," I said, looking forward to being alone with him.

Sean turned on the radio, and Twisted Sister blasted out from all four speakers. He quickly pressed the scan button on the radio until it stopped at a more mellow station.

I smiled gratefully. Sean knew I hated heavy metal, and I appreciated his making the sacrifice for me.

"It's a good thing L.A. has so many stations to choose from," Sean said.

"You're righ-tt," The second word came out like a yelp as I was struck with a violent pain in my side.

"Is something wrong?" Sean asked, his voice full of concern.

"It's nothing," I lied.

I was worried. I'd woken up the night before

with a shooting pain in my right side. But it had passed fairly quickly, and I soon fell asleep again. During the day I'd felt a few more painful twinges, but I didn't want to miss the party, so I ignored them.

But there was no way I could ignore the next stab of pain. It felt as if someone were sticking me in the side with a six-inch dagger. "Ow," I screamed.

"Hey, Gretch, what's wrong?" He looked so upset that I felt his attention alone might be enough to cure me. The pain subsided. "Oh, nothing," I managed to say.

"If it happens again, you're going straight to the doctor," he cautioned. "I really hope you're OK; I've planned on doing lots of dancing tonight."

"I'm as ready as you are," I responded. "Sean, do you remember our first junior high dance?"

"I don't remember dancing with you, if that's what you mean."

"You didn't. In fact, you ducked Melinda and me the entire night. We were sure you were embarrassed that you had had to come to the dance with us."

"I did that?" Sean sounded surprised.

"Yes, you did."

One of the things I loved about dating Sean

was that he and I had a history. We'd known each other for so long that our relationship had been comfortable right from the start. In fact, on our first real date we spent hours dredging up some of the more outrageous incidents from our past. He reminded me of the time I tried to give myself a home permanent and ended up looking like an actor from a horror movie. I brought up the time Sean decided to surprise his mother by making dinner, but they wound up having to order in a pizza after the hamburgers he made came out looking like pieces of charcoal. By the time we'd finished, I realized I'd never laughed so hard in my life.

Just then another stab in my side interrupted my thoughts. I think I turned green. I know I felt green. When Sean turned to look at me again, he gasped. "God, Gretchen, you look awful."

"I feel like I'm dying," I moaned. "I think you'd better get me to the hospital."

I must have put a real scare into Sean because he made a quick U-turn on the narrow road. Stepping on the gas, he raced across town toward Brimley Medical Center.

was [illegible] he [illegible] [illegible] [illegible]
each time for so long that [illegible] [illegible]
had been comfortable [illegible] from the [illegible] in
fact, on our [illegible] [illegible] [illegible] spectacular,
dredging up some of the many outrageous
incidents from our past. He reminded me of
the time I tried a [illegible] [illegible] [illegible] for a
part and ended up [illegible] [illegible] [illegible]
a [illegible] [illegible] [illegible] up the time [illegible]
[illegible] [illegible] [illegible] [illegible] making [illegible]
[illegible] but they [illegible] [illegible] to [illegible] in a
[illegible] after the [illegible] [illegible] to [illegible] but
[illegible] the [illegible] [illegible] [illegible] the [illegible]
[illegible] [illegible]. I realized I'd been [illegible] so
[illegible] to my life.

Just then another [illegible] my [illegible] [illegible]
[illegible] [illegible] I [illegible] green [illegible]
[illegible] [illegible] from [illegible] [illegible] to [illegible]
[illegible] [illegible] [illegible]. "God, [illegible] you
look awful."

"I feel like I'm dying," I [illegible]. "[illegible]
[illegible] [illegible] at the hospital."

"I [illegible] have [illegible] [illegible] [illegible] Stan
[illegible] [illegible] I [illegible] the [illegible]
[illegible] on the [illegible] he [illegible] across
town to [illegible] Medical Center.

Chapter Two

The first thing I remembered after Sean carried me into the emergency room was waking up the next morning in a hospital bed. I was wearing a white gown with tiny blue flowers on it and a big *B* stamped on the front. The needle in my arm was connected by a tube to a bottle, which hung above my head on a metal pole. Through the tube a clear liquid was dripping into my body.

I felt kind of woozy, but at least the awful pain was gone. My side still hurt, however, and I pulled up my gown to look at the incision. I wrinkled my nose in disgust at the surgical staples with which they'd closed up the lower part of my abdomen after removing my appendix. *So much for bikinis this summer*, I thought despairingly.

A little while later a doctor came in to see me. "Good morning, Gretchen," he said, reading my name from the chart at the foot of my bed. "I'm Doctor Benard. How are you feeling today?"

"A lot better than I did last night."

Dr. Benard was kind of cute for an older guy. He was tall and had wavy, dark brown hair, a mustache, and two dimples that showed when he smiled. But it was one of those practiced, fake smiles I'd seen on TV doctors' faces when they're trying to tell their patients they're dying. It got me nervous. "Hey, I'm not going to die, am I?" I asked.

His smile turned into a chuckle. "Of course not, Gretchen. But from the looks of it, you got here just in time. A few hours longer and that appendix of yours would have burst. But don't worry. You're going to be all right now."

"When can I go home?"

"Whoa," he said, putting his hand out as if to stop me. "You've got some recovering to do first. But if all goes well, we ought to be able to send you home in three or four days."

"Four days!" I would have shouted the words, but I was still weak from the operation.

"The time will go faster than you think. The nurse will be in soon to show you how to operate the TV and to walk you around a little. And I'll give the OK to let your friends come visit."

I'd been in this hospital only once before,

and I hadn't liked it. I'd gone with Melinda to visit a friend who'd injured his knee in a football game. His room had been just like the one I was in. The wall to my right was made up of windows covered by the most awful brown, orange, and yellow flowered drapes I'd ever seen. The TV was mounted on the wall in front of me, and a dresser stood below it. Next to the dresser was the door to the bathroom. Right next to that was a large door to the outside world, and next to the left wall was another bed. It was empty. I didn't even have a roommate to keep me company.

Fortunately, I didn't have time to start feeling really sorry for myself. Shortly after Dr. Benard left, my parents came to visit me. Mom was carrying a large basket of multicolored tulips and had a big, cheery smile on her face. As soon as she saw me, the smile disappeared. "Oh, Gretchen," she cried as she leaned over the bed rail. "My poor baby." She kissed me and stroked my cheeks the way she had when I was younger.

Poor Mom, I thought, *she looks so tired*. She must have been there all night, worrying about me. "I'll be OK, Mom," I reassured her. "The doctor said so."

"You should have told me you were in pain," Mom said. "That's what mothers are for."

"I know. I thought it'd go away," I explained.

"That's not important now," Dad said, pulling up a chair. "The important thing is that you're going to be all right."

"I'm glad you're here, Daddy," I said. "When did you get back?"

"A few hours ago. When I heard you were sick, I hopped on the first plane I could get." My father runs two printing plants, one here in Los Angeles, the other one in San Diego. He'd been down at the San Diego plant for the past several days.

"I'm glad you came."

"We're here for you. We want you to know that," Dad said.

I smiled. "I know that, Dad."

They stayed for a little while longer. Before they left Mom said, "We'll be back this evening with your robe and some pajamas. Is there anything else you'd like us to bring from home?"

I shook my head, and they started to walk toward the door. "Oh, there is one thing," I called after them. "Uh, could you bring my Pooh bear? It's—"

"I know where it is," Mom said.

"I—uh, I just want to have something familiar to look at," I explained.

Mom smiled, and I could tell that she understood. She knew how scared I was and how comforting an old friend like Pooh could be.

"Oh, Gretchen," Mom added as they opened the door to leave. "Sean's waiting to see you. Try to keep the visit short. You need your rest," she told me. "We'll be back later. Bye now."

"Bye," I said.

As soon as my parents left, the door opened again. Sean looked as if he hadn't got much sleep, but it was great to see him. "Come on in," I said.

He came over to the bed and kissed me gently on the forehead. "Don't worry, Gretch. You're going to be out of here in no time," he said. His usual enthusiasm hadn't been dampened by his lack of sleep.

"The doctor said I'll have to be here for four days," I told him.

He looked so disappointed. "Yeah, I don't like it much either," I continued. "But at least I'll never have to ruin another date by getting appendicitis again."

"I'm glad to see you still have your sense of humor," he said. "But the important thing is that you're going to get better."

"You sound like my father," I said. "And you look tired."

"That's because I was here half the night.

After I brought you here, I called your mom and waited with her while the doctors examined you. I think she was glad to have me around. So I stayed until you were in the recovery room. By that point your dad had gotten here, and they told me to go home and get some rest. But I had to come back to see how you're doing."

"I'm so glad you did," I said, squeezing his hand.

He bent down and kissed me again. "That was from everyone who told me to tell you to get better soon."

"Who did you tell?"

"You know Melinda. She couldn't keep quiet about this. Anyway, she said that Lindsay said the party wasn't the same without us."

"I'm sorry you had to miss it, too."

"It was probably a bore. Anyway, Melinda said she'll come see you tomorrow. I've got to go now, too. I promised your mom I wouldn't stay too long."

"That's OK. I understand," I said.

Just then a nurse named Ms. Halstead barged in and informed me that it was time for me to have my walk. Hastily Sean and I said our goodbyes as Ms. Halstead lowered my bed rails.

"Up and at 'em," she barked harshly.

As I stood up, I understood for the first time what "sea legs" meant. I felt as if I were being asked to balance on a floor made of Jell-O. The pictures lining the walls seemed to rise and fall as if they were bobbing in water. But the nurse wouldn't give me a break. "You've got to start walking," she insisted.

The IV was on a portable stand, and she moved it over beside me. Then she led me to the bathroom and back again, her arm steadying me only slightly. The whole process was terribly disorienting. My head buzzed, my legs felt weak, and I didn't think I'd make it.

But somehow I did.

"Now, that wasn't too bad, was it?" Ms. Halstead asked.

From the comfort of my bed, the short walk didn't seem so terrible. "No," I admitted.

"I'll be back to walk you around later. We've got to keep you active," she said.

Soon after the nurse left, I dozed off. When I awoke, I was still feeling a little woozy. But later that afternoon my head had cleared considerably, and I felt as good as ever. With no one to keep me company and nothing interesting to watch on TV, I was ready to climb the walls.

Worst of all, I was starving. I hadn't eaten all day, and even though I'd heard hospital food was terrible, I would have gladly traded anything for a tuna sandwich. When I asked Ms. Halstead when I could eat, she said that my chart indicated I couldn't have anything until the following morning.

Still, I didn't think something small would hurt. Maybe an egg or some toast. Gingerly I sat up and swung my legs over the side of the bed, slowly lowering them to the floor. Realizing the IV needle was still in my arm, I pulled it out so it wouldn't get in my way as I began to walk.

My head still felt light, but I remembered seeing a wheelchair folded up in the back of my closet. I took it out, sprang it open, and sat down. A moment later I felt much better. Grabbing my purse from the closet, I wheeled myself out of the room and down the hall to the elevator.

Fortunately no one saw me. And my good fortune held as the elevator came seconds after I pushed the Down button.

I kept willing it to go faster as the image of Ms. Halstead's angry face loomed before my eyes. I managed to get the wheelchair off the elevator and pushed myself as fast as I could to the cafeteria, which I remembered from my earlier visit as being on the first floor.

As soon as I got inside, I found out I'd have

to forego any hot food. The cafeteria was closed between lunch and dinner, and the only food available was hot coffee and things from the vending machines lined up along the cafeteria back wall.

Well, even a candy bar was better than nothing, I thought. Taking some change from my purse, I dropped it into the machine and pressed the button for a granola bar.

Nothing happened. In frustration I began to pound the machine with my fists. But I was too weak to do anything besides make my hands sore.

"Hey, what's going on here?"

Uh-oh, they've caught me, I thought. Sheepishly I turned around to look at my captor.

But it wasn't a guard or an orderly. Standing behind me was a boy about my age dressed in pajamas and a red flannel robe. He smiled at me, but it was nothing like Dr. Benard's pseudo-smile. This guy just looked friendly.

"Hi," I said, smiling back. "The machine ate my money."

"That's too bad," he said, studying both the machine and me in turn. A moment later he reached inside the coin return slot and pulled out my change. "Is this yours?" he asked.

Without waiting for an answer, he dropped it back into the machine. "Now, which one did you want?"

I pointed to the granola bar, and my good samaritan friend pressed the button and retrieved it for me. "Thanks, um—"

"Mitch. Mitch Gantry," he said awkwardly, offering me his left hand. He looked apologetically at his right arm, which was encased in a cast. "I know you're supposed to shake with your right hand, but as you can see, mine is temporarily out of commission."

"I see. I'm Gretchen Diamond," I said, shaking his healthy hand.

He grinned. "Nice wheels," he commented, pointing to the wheelchair.

"Aren't they?" I responded. "What did you do to your arm?"

"I got into a little accident. I hit my head, too, so they're keeping me in here for observation. What about you?"

"I got my appendix out." I sighed. "Great place to spend the weekend, huh?"

Mitch leaned against the candy machine, enabling me to get a good look at his handsome, angular face. He looked a little like Matt Dillon. It wasn't so much that he had the same black hair and dark brooding eyes, but that he had Matt's expressions.

I started to unwrap the granola bar Mitch had placed in my hand when he turned to me. "When'd you get here?" he asked.

"Last night. Can you believe they haven't given me anything to eat?"

"Didn't you say you got your appendix out?" he asked.

"Yeah."

"Just last night?" he asked in surprise. "Aren't you supposed to be hooked up to an IV?"

"Hey, are you a doctor or something?"

"No, but my kid brother got his appendix out last year. He had an IV for days."

"I took it out," I said nonchalantly, lifting the granola bar to my mouth.

Looking at me in shock, Mitch snatched the bar from my hand. "Wait. You can't eat that!" he yelled.

"Give it back," I cried. "You can't do this to me."

"It's for your own good," he said.

"How do you know? You just said you're not a doctor."

"I know enough to know you're in no condition to eat that."

"Please let me have it," I begged.

"No."

"Monster!" I cried. I got out of the chair and made a grab at Mitch's arm.

He stepped back. "Believe me, no matter how much you want to eat this right now, it'll only make you sicker."

I didn't want to admit it to him, but I was feeling very weak. Leaning against the candy machine for support, I made one last appeal. "I don't care. I want it anyway."

"No." He put the bar in his robe pocket.

"Then get out of here. I never want to see you again!" I was about to yell something else at him when I passed out.

Chapter Three

I don't know how long I was out, but when I woke up, everything was neatly back in its place. The pillows were propped under my head, and the IV was inserted securely in my arm. Several layers of tape were wrapped around the needle to make sure I didn't rip it off again. But I wasn't stupid enough to make the same mistake twice. I felt terrible, and I'd learned my lesson.

I was also feeling pretty groggy, even worse than I had after I'd first awakened from the operation. I might have turned around and gone right back to sleep if Ms. Halstead hadn't been standing beside me. That ugly stare of hers was enough to keep anyone awake.

"Uh, what time is it?" I asked. My voice was scarcely above a whisper even though I was trying to talk normally.

"Eight o'clock," she said curtly.

Well, at least I hadn't been out too long. It had been midafternoon when I'd ventured downstairs. But why did it look so light outside?

Ms. Halstead must have seen my confusion as I turned my head to the window. "In the morning," she added. "What on earth was in your mind, traipsing around the hospital without permission?"

I knew that I should act sorry, but Ms. Halstead's know-it-all superior manner made me furious. "Oh, just taking a stroll," I replied as coolly as I could.

"A girl in your condition ought to know better," she continued as if she hadn't heard me. "All you've done is to set back your own recovery. You're lucky your friend was with you when you passed out. He got help for you right away."

Friend? Who was she talking about? The previous night's events were a blur. Slowly I remembered Mitch, the boy at the candy machine.

I smiled as I thought about him. I'd been so mad when he'd snatched that candy bar away from me. But he'd been absolutely right.

The guy probably thought I was really dumb. But he hadn't understood how desperate I'd been. In fact, *I* was even finding it hard to believe how reckless I'd been. The nurse was right—I should have known better. Lying back on my pillow, I felt a surge of nausea.

"Now you should get some rest," Ms. Halstead said as she adjusted my IV. "The doctor will be in to see you soon."

It was more like four hours later when Dr. Benard arrived. His smile was gone. "What were you trying to do, kill yourself?" he asked angrily.

"I know. I know. I'll never do it again. I swear," I said.

"I feel like tying your hands to the bed to keep you here, but, of course, I won't," he said, obviously still annoyed. He went on lecturing me like that for quite some time.

"I swear I'll never do it again," I promised him.

"Good," he said at last. "I want you to continue to get up and around, build your strength. Then we'll see how you're doing in a few days."

"Yes, Doctor," I said obediently.

Needless to say, I felt lousy after he left. While I was lying there feeling terribly sorry for myself, my parents came in. I must have looked awful because I could see their smiles fading as they approached my bed.

"My God, Gretchen, how could you have done such a thing?" my father scolded.

"So, Doctor Benard told you everything."

"He certainly did," Dad said. "When we got here last night to see you." He must have seen the remorse in my eyes, because he didn't continue the lecture. "Just don't do it again," he said quietly.

"I brought your things," Mom said. "Actually, I brought them last night, but you were sound asleep, and I didn't want to leave them. So I took them home and brought them back again." She put my lavender weekend bag on the bedside table. She opened it and put a couple of nightgowns in the closet. I was glad to see she'd brought along my makeup kit, though I was in no condition to do anything about my appearance. On my last trip to the bathroom, I had been horrified to see big, dark blotches under my eyes and pasty white cheeks beneath them. I looked like something from a fright show.

Without comment Mom then took Pooh out and put him next to me on the bed. Then she opened her purse. "I picked up some puzzle books and magazines downstairs," she said, handing them to me.

"Thanks, Mom," I said as I gave my old bear a hug.

They stayed for a while. I'm not sure how long because I dozed off. When I awoke they were gone.

It was eerie. The drapes were open a little, and the late-afternoon sun cast long shadows across the room. Outside the partially opened door, I could hear and see the rest of the world passing by. I pressed the button that raised my bed until I was sitting almost straight up and clutched Pooh to my side. *Somehow we'll get through this*, I told my old friend.

I put on the TV, more to have some noise in the room than for any real entertainment. I found an old movie that wasn't too bad and was just starting to get into it when there was a knock at the door. "Hey, Gretch, it's me."

I would have recognized Sean's voice anywhere. He was standing just outside the door, and I quickly called, "Come in."

Sean pushed the door open all the way. The last remnants of a candy bar were in his hands. My stomach gurgled in agony.

"Gretchen, what happened to you? You look awful."

I knew he meant well, even if he didn't sound as if he did.

"Didn't you hear? I took a little walk yesterday." I gave him an abbreviated rundown.

"I'll bet the doctor really gave it to you," he said when I finished.

"And my parents. You want to add anything?" I asked.

"No way," he said. "I'm sure you've had enough lectures for one day."

He leaned over and gave my nose a kiss. "Besides, I want to keep you happy and away from strange guys who hang around vending machines."

I looked at Sean in surprise. "Sean Flanders, you sound jealous!"

"Who, me?" he asked innocently as he lowered the rail on my bed and sat down next to me. Taking the television control, he spun it until he found a sports channel.

"Well, you've got nothing to worry about," I assured him. "He was just some guy. I'll probably never see him again."

Sean didn't say another word about it. Instead, he settled in to watch a game. As far as I was concerned, it was a dead issue, too, but just to make sure he really understood, I slipped my hand into his and gave it a big squeeze.

We spent a pleasant few hours watching TV, enjoying just being together. Having him there made me feel so much better I wished there were a way he could stay longer. But, of course, there wasn't.

"OK, Gretchen, it's time for your sponge bath. Young man, please step outside for a moment."

I groaned. It seemed like one of the nurses or nurse's aides was always barging in.

Sean looked helplessly at me. "I think it's time I left," he said. I could see he was reluctant. "I'll see you tomorrow."

"I'm looking forward to it."

I think Sean might have thought the sponge bath was going to take a long time. But it didn't at all. The aide was obviously an old hand at this type of thing and was finished in only a few minutes. "Now, isn't that better?" she asked.

She was right. "I feel almost human now," I told her.

The woman left, and I was alone again. With nothing better to do, I turned on the TV. After a while there was a knock at my door.

"Come in," I said wearily.

"They said you could have visitors. Is it OK if I come in?"

"Sure, Mitch," I said, shaking my head in wonder. "I never thought I'd see you again."

"So you're glad to see me," he said, more as a statement than a question.

"I guess I am. I thought a lot about what happened yesterday and realize I owe you an apology. I'm glad you're giving me the chance to say I'm sorry."

"Accepted," he said.

I was relieved to see he was smiling. "I figured after the way I treated you, you wouldn't want to have anything to do with me. I guess I was kind of rough," I admitted.

"Oh, that." He shrugged off the incident. "People in hospitals do lots of crazy things—though I have to admit, not many with your determination."

"Have you been in a lot of hospitals?"

"Let's just say I've seen more of the inside of hospitals than most people."

"Why? You look healthy enough to me."

"Oh, I'm not sick or anything. The doctor says the arm's going to be fine, too. I asked him if that meant I'd be able to play the piano. He said yes, and I told him that was great. I'd never been able to play before."

"God, do you know how old that joke is?" I groaned.

"But I made you smile, right? Works every time. I like to cheer people up. The world is depressing enough."

"Thanks, I needed some cheering up."

He smiled. "I wanted to give you this book.

It's one of my favorites. I figure you're going to go stir crazy in a few more days. It ought to keep you out of trouble."

"Hmm, *Stranger in a Strange Land.*" I examined the thick science fiction novel. "What an appropriate title for this place," I quipped, adding, "Thanks. I've always wanted to read this, but I never had the time."

"You have plenty of time to read now," he said. "And you look to me like the type of person who appreciates a good book."

"I do," I said, surprised. "But how can you tell?"

"Actually, it was a guess." He glanced up at the TV. "I'm not interrupting anything important, am I?"

"No, just some dumb videos—oh, wait a second. There's Bruce Springsteen." I turned up the volume.

"You like him, too?" Mitch asked.

"The Boss is one of my favorites," I replied.

Neither of us said anything as we watched Bruce play. After the song was over, I turned the volume back down and looked at Mitch.

"Tell me more about you. All we've done is talk about me."

"What can I say? I'm sixteen. I'm a junior at Southgate High—I go there because they have such a good fine arts program. I've got two younger brothers and an older sister—and a broken arm."

"An ulna," I added. "I remember that from biology. How'd you get it?"

"I have a part-time job with a gardener. We were trimming the branches on a tree when a limb got away. I tried to duck but lost my footing and took a ten-foot fall. It knocked me out for a while."

"You must be in a lot of pain."

"Not really. I get headaches that come and go. But this cast is driving me crazy. Even if my arm didn't hurt, the cast would keep me from doing things. Guess I'll have to get used to it."

"Maybe it'd help if your cast was decorated," I said. "Mind if I try?"

"Be my guest." He pulled a blue, felt-tipped pen from his robe pocket, then rested his cast on the sliding table over my bed. I wrote "Gretchen was here" in my big, flowery script.

"Hey, you're a lefty!" he cried.

"What about it?" I challenged.

He smiled. "I am, too," he cried. "Lucky I broke my right arm."

"You said that you go to Southgate because of art," I said. "Tell me about it."

"Well," he said shyly, "I'd like to be an architect. I want to build houses. My favorite is one

I designed to look out over the Valley. It's set into the hill and juts out like a giant piece of pie. It's got a round living room and curved windows and lots of skylights." He paused. "And of course a swimming pool and a sauna."

"It sounds a little like my friend Lindsay's house," I said.

Mitch looked crestfallen. "She stole my house?"

"Don't let it bother you. The house is gorgeous."

"I like to draw, too," he continued. "Especially with charcoal."

"Can you do a sketch of these tulips?" I asked, pointing to the flowers.

"I've got a better idea," Mitch said. He got up and walked over to the unoccupied bed next to mine. He removed the paper mat from underneath the empty water pitcher and cup on the bedside tray. "My canvas," he said jokingly as he sat down at the foot of my bed.

I gave him back his pen, and he began to draw. "I've been monopolizing the conversation," he said. "Now tell me about you."

"Well, I go to school, same as you. I'm a cheerleader for Brimley High. I also run girls' track." I winced. "Guess I won't be doing either for a while."

"You might be forced to concentrate on schoolwork," Mitch said jokingly.

"I don't mind. Schoolwork comes pretty easily to me. Biology's my favorite. I think I'd like to go into research someday. I've even been working on an extracredit project on genetics—about the effects of nature versus nurture."

"Tell me about it," Mitch said.

"Maybe later. I'm too tired to get into it now."

"Well," he said, getting up, "I hope you've got the energy to look at this." He handed me the sketch he'd been working on.

The picture in front of me was of a smiling girl with shoulder-length, wavy hair and sparkling eyes. It was a fair rendition of what I looked like before I came to the hospital.

I was amazed. "But that's not what I look like!" I exclaimed. "I'm a wreck!"

"That's not what I see," he said.

"You're really sweet to have drawn this," I said. "May I keep it?"

To my surprise, Mitch shook his head. "I want to keep it for myself," he said.

Suddenly I got a weird sensation in my stomach. "Uh, Mitch, I think there's something you ought to know. I've got a boyfriend."

"I guess that means you won't want me visiting you again."

"No, not at all. I want to be your friend, but I just thought you should know where I stand. I've really enjoyed your visit."

"I'm glad to hear that. I figured someone determined enough to have crawled out of her hospital bed for a candy bar was somebody worth seeing again. Mind if I stop by tomorrow?"

"As a matter of fact, Doctor Benard wants me to walk around as much as I can. If you've got nothing else to do tomorrow, would you take me for a walk?"

"Sounds great. I'll see you then," he said. He patted my arm with his good hand, then picked up the sketch he'd drawn.

"Won't you let me keep it?" I pressed.

"Afraid not," he said with the tiniest trace of a grin. "I kind of like it. I'm going to put it in my portfolio."

I had a feeling that I was going to like having Mitch for a friend.

Chapter Four

Television is a great time passer in the hospital, and the next morning I tuned in. I didn't see any point in watching a soap opera because I wouldn't be able to follow it when I got home, so I ended up watching game shows. There was one in particular that I liked called "Moneymaker." I hate to admit it, but I got into that one because one of the contestants was a really gorgeous college guy. But he turned out to be as stupid as he was good-looking. He disappointed me so much that I turned off the TV in disgust. I had no desire to tackle the puzzle books Mom left for me, so I picked up Mitch's book.

The plot was so complicated that it took me awhile to get the situation straight in my head. But once I did, I was fascinated. I put it down only when Ms. Halstead came in for one of her periodic visits to help me out of bed.

I was still reading when there was a knock on my door several hours later. This time Mitch didn't even wait for me to say "come in."

"Hey, they took out your IV!" he said excitedly. "How does it feel to be a free woman?"

"It's too early to tell. They just took it away an hour ago. But it's good to know I'll be getting real food at last!"

"If you want, I'll go down and get you something."

"No, thanks," I said, laughing. "I think this time I'll wait until they're ready to feed me."

"I'm glad you're feeling better," he said. "And I see you started the book, too. How do you like it?"

"It's terrific." I rested the book facedown on my lap. "I'm kind of surprised a guy like you would be into reading. You don't seem the type."

Mitch grinned. "Oh? What is the type, a skinny nerd with acne and buck teeth?" Plopping down on my bed, Mitch tried his best to look like the nerd he'd described. It made me laugh. "That's what we like to see," he continued. "Anyway, I like to read because it's like entering another world. It can take you to faraway places and make you forget your surroundings."

I nodded. "And it sure beats watching TV."

"I know what you mean." Mitch flashed me a knowing smile. "Are you ready for your workout?"

I took hold of his outstretched hand, grateful for the assistance, and eased out of bed. "The way you said that, I feel as if I should be wearing my sweats instead of a nightgown." I slipped into my well worn but very comfortable mauve velour robe.

"You look just fine," he said.

I didn't know how he could say that. I hadn't washed my hair in two days and wasn't wearing any makeup, though the dark blotches under my eyes were gone. But I accepted his compliment, grateful that I could show my rumpled self without repulsing the world.

Slowly we made our way out of the room and walked toward the nurses' station down the corridor.

"Hey, I got some good news today," Mitch said as we walked. "The X rays they took of my head came back negative. The doctor told me this morning. He seemed so happy for me, but I don't know why he was so excited. I could have told him there was nothing wrong with me."

"Well, you did take a pretty bad fall."

"I guess it just goes to prove I've got a real hard head."

"So will you be going home today?"

He sighed. "Afraid not. Even though the tests were negative, they want to keep me here for another day or so."

I could hear the disappointment in his voice. "Believe me, I know what you mean," I grumbled. "I can't wait to get out of here either. It's no place for a teenager."

"For anyone," he added. "They feed you dinner at five in the afternoon, they come around to take your temperature at the worst possible moments, and they only allow you visitors when *they* say."

"Welcome to prison," I added.

Mitch pointed to one of the paintings on the wall next to us. I was glad for the chance to stop for a minute. This postoperative walking *was* hard work. "And here's another example of the hospital's stupidity. They go to all the trouble of getting paintings to decorate the place, but instead of hanging something decent, they put up garbage like that."

"I know what you mean," I agreed. "It looks like something that came from one of those paint-by-number kits. But, on the other hand, good art costs a lot of money."

"Not necessarily. This bank near our school showcases work done by Southgate students. And it doesn't cost them a dime."

"Hmmm. Sounds like a great idea. Have they used your stuff?" I asked.

Mitch shrugged his shoulders. "Naw, I'm not that good. I'm more into my architecture." Mitch stopped walking. "Well, you made it to the nurses' station."

I was still in one piece, but I was ready to turn back. "You don't have to walk me back to my room if you don't want to. I think if I hold on to the wall I'll do just fine."

"I'm sure you will, but I signed on for a round trip."

"You sure you don't mind?"

"Of course not."

As we headed back, I looked into a few of the other rooms. Each one had the same ugly drapes that were in my room. "Speaking of art, Mitch, I have a suggestion for you. If you ever build a hospital, find a decorator who has better taste in drapes."

"I've got the same kind in my room. Don't you like them?"

"No, I hate them. They're the worst-looking flowers I've ever seen. I think whoever designed them must need glasses."

"Oh, I think they're kind of funky. And who knows? Maybe the guy's nearsighted. They say that Van Gogh might have been. And just

think what the world would have lost if someone had given him a pair of glasses."

Quite frankly I didn't know because I'd never seen a Van Gogh. But I was impressed with Mitch's knowledge and didn't want to admit my ignorance.

We reached my room, and Mitch walked me to the bed. "Thanks a lot for helping me out," I said. "I can't wait to tell Sean that I'm recovering."

"Sean?"

"My boyfriend."

"You must like him a lot."

"I do."

"What's he like?" Mitch sat down on the bed to listen.

"Well, he's a little over six feet tall. He's got blond hair and hazel eyes, and he plays forward on our basketball team."

"What else," Mitch prodded.

I thought for a moment. "He's got a great sense of humor. He's always pulling pranks. We haven't been dating that long, but we do the usual things—see movies, party with friends, that kind of stuff."

"I'll bet he's really proud of you and your genetics project."

"I haven't really told him much about it."

"Doesn't he care about your interests?"

"Sure. We always share the important stuff. I guess I just forgot to tell him." I started to feel uncomfortable with the way the conversation was going. "You know, Mitch, I've known Sean practically my whole life, and I've wanted to go out with him for almost as long. It's like a dream come true. And to top that off, his twin sister is my best friend."

Just then there was a knock on the door. "Gretchen, can we come in?"

"I'd better get going," said Mitch. He slid off the bed and headed for the door. "I'll see you tomorrow," he called. As he left he gave my friends a friendly smile.

"Surprise!" In walked Melinda and my friends Betsy and Clare. Clare handed me a giant envelope. "Open it," she said eagerly.

Inside was a huge get-well card, signed by all of my friends. Even a few of my teachers had signed it. "Thanks, guys," I said, smiling.

When I glanced up from the card, Clare and Betsy were looking at me, but Melinda was staring at the door. "That's just Mitch. He's a patient here, too," I said.

"He's cute," Betsy said.

"Yes, I guess he is," I answered. Of course, I was well aware of Mitch's good looks. "If you like, I'll give him your phone number."

Betsy began to search through her purse for

a pen. Never mind, I know it," I said, laughing. "Gee, it's great to see you guys."

"Everybody at school hopes you get out of here soon," Clare said.

"Me, too," I said. "If I'm here too much longer, I'll go crazy."

Melinda plopped down on my bed. "Yeah, I'll bet you're getting pretty bored, huh?"

"Well, Mitch helped me exercise this wretched body of mine. That was a nice change. Otherwise, it's been nothing but a boring day of TV," I said. "At least Mitch was thoughtful enough to provide me with this book to read."

Melinda looked at the title. "Sean had to read that in school. He said it put him to sleep."

"Well, I like it. Now, is anyone going to tell me about Lindsay's party? I think I can handle the agony of having missed it."

"You didn't miss much," Betsy said, sitting down on the opposite side of the bed from Melinda. "The food was pretty lousy, and the band didn't play anything you could dance to."

Clare gave Betsy a funny look. "She doesn't care about that stuff," she said, running her fingers through her hair the way she always did. She turned to me. "Lance Robbins was his usual jerky self. Lindsay even made him leave when he started acting rowdy. She was afraid he was going to break something." Clare paused for effect. "But the big surprise of the night was when Alice English arrived with Hank Seeff. She said she's through with Billy forever. And she was definitely acting very cozy with Hank."

"And as soon as they let you leave this place," Melinda told me, "I'm going to throw a party for you."

"Melinda, that's great," I said. "It's just what I need—more incentive to get out of here as soon as I can."

"Glad to be of service," she answered.

I leaned forward. "But if you guys really want to do something for me, could you help me wash this?" I held up a strand of limp, dirty hair. "I can't shower yet, and it's hard in the sink. I'd like to look presentable when Sean comes later."

Clare stood up and picked up her purse. "Leave it to me," she said.

Clare did a good job. And Melinda pitched in by taking my makeup kit and going to work on my face. The part of my body from the neck up was getting back to normal.

Sean came to visit later that evening. I hadn't realized how much I'd missed him until he was actually there. He looked so adorable in his faded blue sportshirt and tan cords. His hair was windblown, and he looked very boyish.

"How are you, buddy?" I asked him.

"The important thing is how you are. I missed you today, Gretch," he said.

"You hardly ever see me in school—except for study hall."

"But it wasn't the same without you." He kissed me lightly. "When are they springing you?"

"I still don't know. I feel pretty good lying down, but I feel a little woozy every time they make me get up and walk around."

"You'll probably get over that soon," he said. Changing the subject, Sean asked, "You know old Mrs. Rossner, my Spanish teacher, right?"

"Yeah, she's the one who looks like a bird—especially her nose."

Sean nodded. "Well, today in class Scott Johnson drew this cartoon of her eating birdseed from a feeder. He drew feathers all over her, and—get this—he also drew her corrective shoes. But she caught us passing the drawing around the class. Gretchen, you should have seen the look on her face when she looked at the cartoon and realized it was a picture of herself."

"Poor lady," I said. I could feel her embarrassment, but I knew Sean must have been laughing hysterically at the sight.

"But here's the really funny part," he continued. "She went on with the lesson without missing a beat. I practically split my gut, trying not to laugh. But none of us said a word. She went through the entire period pretending nothing had happened."

"That's a lot more exciting than what went on here. About the only interesting thing was when Ms. Halstead came in and took out the IV from my arm. I'm free." I waved my left arm in the air.

"That's nice," he said a bit indifferently.

"Don't you know what that means? I got to eat a real dinner tonight. It was mostly bland, liquidy stuff like soup and applesauce, but it was real food."

"Good for you."

"I've also got something to show you." I held up the jar that was on my bedstand.

Sean wrinkled his nose. "What's that?"

"It's my appendix. I asked Doctor Benard what they did with it after they took it out. He told me that they sent it down to pathology to check it out and make sure it wasn't cancerous or anything like that. I asked him if I could have it, and he said yes. Fascinating, isn't it?"

The blood drained out of Sean's face. "I guess that's one way of putting it."

"You're not impressed, I can tell. Well," I added lightly, "that's OK. You're not the one who plans to be a scientist."

"Now I know why," he said with disgust. But just as quickly, he brightened. "So, did Melinda tell you about the party for you?"

"You going to be there?" I asked.

"Of course—it's at my house!" He grinned, but then his voice softened. "You know I wouldn't miss it."

"I know. But it's always nice to hear."

"You're a hopeless romantic, Gretch," he said.

"And proud of it," I added.

"In that case I have some bad news. I'm not going to be able to come see you tomorrow. I've got practice in the afternoon and a game tomorrow night. And sometime in between the two, I've got to take Baby to the car wash."

"Who're we playing?"

"Jefferson. Should be a snap."

"I'm going to miss seeing you," I said.

"Me, too," he agreed, softly kissing me.

Chapter Five

"Oh, Mitch, you shouldn't have," I cried.

Mitch came in the next day, carrying a huge bunch of flowers. It was a really pretty arrangement of multicolored daisies with five pink balloons nestled right above the petals. "They're so extravagant, Mitch."

"What's the matter? Don't you like them?"

Mitch looked like a wistful little boy when he frowned. He must have known that all he had to do was look at me like that and I'd melt. "Oh, no," I said. "They're beautiful. But you shouldn't have gone to the trouble. They look so expensive."

"I'm not very good at lying. I suppose I could get away with it, but I wouldn't feel right about it."

"Don't tell me you stole them!" I gasped.

"No. On my way to see you yesterday, I saw these flowers sitting on a table near the nurses' station. They were there today, too. So I asked one of the nurses on duty who they were for, and she told me that the woman had checked out yesterday afternoon and didn't want them. She said I could have them."

"Thank you," I said.

"Besides," he continued, "yesterday you sounded so down about those drapes. I thought you thought the room could use some brightening up."

"I'll say," I agreed.

Mitch put the flowers next to my tulips and Pooh, who was resting on the bedside table. "So is this from Sean?" he questioned.

"No," I said. "I've had Pooh since I was five. My dad brought him home from one of his business trips."

"He sounds a little like Pete," he said.

"Who's that?"

"Pete's not a who, he's a what. Pete's the name I gave this blanket I had when I was a kid. I used to drag it with me wherever I went. My parents tried everything to make me get rid of it. But one day I just stopped carrying Pete around."

He clasped his hands together. "Well, you ready for your walk?"

I nodded. "I'm never going to get up to running speed if I don't get up and move around."

"Want some help?" Mitch asked, holding out his hand.

"No, I can do it myself," I said. Confidently but slowly, I lifted up the sheet and pulled my robe around me as I stood up. It made me a little dizzier than I'd expected, so I stopped to rest. A few seconds later I looked up at him and winked. "All set."

"Here, take my arm," he said, offering me his left arm for support.

I looped my arm through his, and together we started to walk toward the door. I suddenly realized I'd been very rude. Turning my head toward Rachel, the woman who'd moved into the bed next to mine that morning, I said, "I'm sorry, Rachel. Allow me to introduce Mitch, my walking cane."

"Hmmm, that's got to be the most unusual introduction I've ever gotten," Mitch said. "Nice to meet you."

"Pleasure's mine," Rachel said.

"It's really nice having a roommate," I added. "Rachel works for one of the movie studios. Just the other day she ate lunch with Eddie Murphy. Isn't that exciting?"

"I didn't eat at the same table *with* him," Rachel said, correcting me. "We were in the same commissary. I do special effects, so I usually don't come into contact with any of the big stars."

"Well, it still sounds exciting to me. I'd like to hear more later, but right now Mitch is going to take me for a spin around the floor. I'll be back soon."

"Take your time," Rachel said.

After we got out into the hallway, Mitch said, "You lucked out there. My roommate's a real bore. He was in a car accident, and all he wants to talk about is how he's going to get the guy who ruined his car."

"Sounds like what Sean would be like if anyone so much as touched his car." Then I said in a teasing tone, "So you only came to see me so you'd have an excuse to leave your room."

"Yup," Mitch said. The smile returned, but it was more forced now. "So how is Sean?"

"Fine, I guess," I said.

"Haven't you seen him?"

"I won't today."

"Something wrong?"

"No, it's just basketball season. He's got practice this afternoon, and there's a game tonight, so it's hard for him to come over."

"You must miss him," Mitch said.

"I guess I do. I'm glad they put Rachel in with me; I enjoy the company."

"What's she in the hospital for?"

I tried to be serious, but I couldn't help myself. "She's having a tummy tuck tomorrow morning," I told him through my giggles.

"What's a tummy tuck?" he asked.

"They surgically remove the fat she can't take off by herself."

"People actually do that?" Mitch asked in amazement.

I nodded. "I've read about it in magazines, but Rachel's the first person I've met who's actually doing it. I guess people will do anything to make themselves look better. I guess you have to be a girl to understand."

"Hey, I've got an older sister. Believe me, I understand." Mitch looked at me and smiled. I looked up and realized we were at the nurses' station. Mitch looked as surprised as I was. I'd been too involved in the conversation to notice how far we'd gone so quickly. "Do you want to go back to your room?"

"No, I'm feeling great. Let's keep going," I said. "You seem to know this place better than I do. Got any ideas?"

A sly smile spread across Mitch's face. "I know of this great cafeteria. They have these vending machines—"

"Forget it!" I shouted. "I'm not going near there again as long as I live."

Mitch thought for a moment, then said, "Think you can make it around the corner?"

"What's around the corner?"

"The patients' lounge. Haven't you discovered it yet?"

I shook my head.

"Well, what are we waiting for?" Mitch asked. "Let's go."

The room took up one corner of the hospital floor and had big windows across two walls, letting in more sunlight than I'd seen in days. There were a few sofas and chairs, some tables topped with piles of magazines, a large aquarium, and over in one corner an old spinet piano. "Let's go over there." I pointed.

Gratefully I eased myself onto the wooden piano bench. Leaning on the music rack, I rested my head on my hands, just above the yellowed keys.

"That was quite a workout," Mitch said. "But you made it."

I raised one fist weakly in the air. "Yay, me," I said weakly.

"I could take you over to that sofa. It'd be more comfortable," Mitch said.

"No, I'll be all right in a minute."

Mitch didn't say a word as he wandered around the room, giving me time to regain my strength. When I finally looked up, he was staring out the window. He looked lost in thought, and I couldn't help but wonder what he was thinking about.

I looked down at the piano keys and played a scale with my left hand. I'm not a great piano player or anything, but I've had lessons for years. The piano didn't sound that great, either, but at least it was relatively in tune. Getting my fingers back in shape, I began to play.

The music snapped Mitch out of his day-dream, and he walked back over. "You didn't tell me you could play the piano," he said, surprised.

"Why did you think I sat here?" Using both hands I started to play an old folk song.

After I finished one stanza of the song, Mitch chimed in. " 'Michael, row your boat ashore, hallelujah. Michael, row your boat ashore, hallelujah.' "

"You've got a nice voice," I said. "Where'd you learn how to sing like that?"

He shrugged. "Just comes naturally, I guess. I did some singing in my school choir when I was little. Say, do you know this one? 'Pretty Woman, walking down the street . . .' "

"Sure, Van Halen," I said. I picked up the key and played the melody while he sang. He kept time by tapping the side of the piano with his hand. When we were done we both clapped. "Bravo!" I said. "You were almost as good as David Lee Roth."

"Thanks. Did you know their version is a remake?"

"Really? Who did the original?"

"A guy named Roy Orbison."

"I didn't know that."

"Yeah. I didn't either till I heard it on the radio once."

"How about this one?" I started to play "Zippety Doo Dah." Mitch picked up on the words, " 'My, oh my, what a wonderful day.' " I sang along this time. I was feeling much better than I had earlier. It felt good to be doing *something* other than vegetating in that bed. Mitch picked up on my rising spirits and requested a few other songs.

We sang "Old MacDonald Had a Farm" and took turns coming up with the animals to sing about. I'd thought of every conceivable farm animal I could and was ready to call it quits. But Mitch didn't want to stop, coming up with " 'And on that farm, he had a zebra—' "

"Hey, Mitch, zebras don't live on farms," I protested.

He dropped his jaw and said, straight-faced, "Don't tell Old MacDonald."

"No fair!"

He continued despite my protest. " 'He had a zebra. Ee, ei, ee, ei, oh. With a—' " He paused. " 'With a—' " He looked lost.

"Well?" I pressed him.

"Er, I don't know what zebras sound like," he admitted sheepishly.

I banged my hands down on the keys and groaned.

"Say, that's the best thing I heard you play all day," he said teasingly.

"Oh, yeah?" I questioned, pretending to be mad. "Let me hear you play!"

All this time he'd been leaning on the piano next to me, but now he sat down beside me. "The only thing I know is this." With his left hand he started to bang out "Chopsticks." The first time around Mitch started on the C and D keys instead of the F and G keys, and it ended up sounding like a bad sound track from a kung fu movie. I couldn't help giggling.

"You think it's so funny, huh, big shot?" he challenged good-naturedly. "Let's see you play the piano with a broken arm."

"Maybe all you need is a quick lesson." Returning my fingers to the keys, I showed him how to play the tune.

"I get it now," he said. "Let me try again."

Mitch played through the melody while I

added some counterpoint of my own. We ran through the song several times, building up speed, until finally we stopped, laughing too hard to go on.

When I recovered I said, "I think we'd better head back to my room. If I laugh any more, I could bust my gut—literally."

"You're right," he said. "But what do you say? Same time tomorrow?"

What *could* I say? "Sure."

When I got back to the room, Rachel took one look at me and gave me one of those know-it-all smiles. "I see you had a good time with your boyfriend."

"He's not here yet," I said without thinking. Then I realized my mistake. "Oh, you mean Mitch? He's not my boyfriend," I corrected her.

Rachel raised her eyebrows at me. "You could have fooled me."

"No, really. I met him here in the hospital. We're just friends."

"It's your life, honey," she said. "I'd sure love to have a guy dote on me the way Mitch does on you. Does he know he's not your boyfriend?"

"Sure," I said. "He knows all about Sean."

But Rachel's words disturbed me. Could she see something I couldn't see? Was I starting to think of Mitch as more than "just a friend"?

Chapter Six

"Boy, am I glad you're here!"

Mitch had been smiling when he'd come by the next afternoon, but my enthusiastic welcome made him light up even more. "Gee, if I'd known you missed me so much, I would have raced here sooner."

"I've been trying to walk around a lot, and it's so boring walking down the halls by myself. I'm glad to have the company."

"I see," Mitch said.

I looked at him strangely. There was something different about him. Then it dawned on me. "Hey, you're wearing street clothes!"

"Yeah, they discharged me a little while ago."

"Then your headaches must be gone."

Mitch nodded. "I'm even used to the cast. It feels like it's always been here."

"That's so great," I said.

"I told my mom I wanted to stay awhile. To help out a friend."

"I'm glad you stopped by. I still have the book you gave me. If you hadn't come back, I wouldn't have known how to return it to you."

"Consider it a present, OK?" He didn't give me a chance to answer. "And take this, too." He reached into the pocket of his baggy army pants and pulled out a granola bar.

"Oh, Mitch," I cried. "I don't believe you."

"I figured you could eat it now. And I didn't think you'd want to go to the cafeteria and get it yourself."

"Thanks." I put the bar on the table. "It reminds me of real-world food. I'd kill for a chili burrito right now."

"You like those, too?" he said. "I think they even have burritos in the cafeteria."

I shook my head. "No, I've got a thing for the ones at Tito's Tacos. Have you ever had them?"

"No, I haven't. Is that a Brimley hangout?"

"Sort of, though lately I haven't gone as much as I'd like." I wrinkled my nose. "Sean hates Mexican food."

"Is there something wrong?"

"It's Sean. He called me from school a little while ago. He was going to come after school, but now he doesn't know if he'll be able to make it at all." I sighed. "Sometimes I hate basketball. It takes up so much of his time."

"And being here only makes it worse for you."

"Yeah. Do you have a girlfriend?"

"Only my sister," he said. "When you don't have a lot of money, it's kind of hard to ask someone out."

"I'm surprised at you," I said in amazement. "I thought you were smart, but I guess you don't understand girls."

He started to protest, but I continued. "Don't you know that money doesn't matter? I'll bet any girl who really liked you would go out with you, even if the date was nothing more than taking a walk down Grant Boulevard."

"You really think so?"

"I'd put money on it," I said firmly.

We ended up back in the lounge at the piano. There were about a half dozen other patients there, quietly reading or talking softly. I didn't want to disturb them by playing something loud, so I tried Chopin's op. 9, no. 2, one of the few classical pieces I knew.

I guess I should use the word "knew" loosely. I don't think anyone ever mangled Chopin as badly.

But Mitch didn't seem to mind. "I'm impressed," he said.

"This is nine years of piano lessons you're hearing. I think I spent about two of them on this piece alone."

"Don't be modest, you're doing a fine job," an older lady put in. She had been sitting in a chair next to the window. Tiny white ringlets framed her round, weather-beaten face. I thought she was still quite pretty, despite her years. "That's lovely," she said. "Play some more."

"I don't know any other classical pieces by heart," I said.

"Well, then, let's see. It may be a little before your time, but do you know, 'As Time Goes By'?"

I smiled. "One of my grandfather's favorite songs."

After the first few bars, Mitch pitched in, too, humming the melody in harmony with my playing. I returned the woman's smile, pleased that she was enjoying the music. After all the fuss people have been making over me, it was nice to be doing something for someone else for a change.

"Oh, thank you," she said as we finished. "You're a very lovely couple."

"Oh, we're just friends," Mitch piped up.

To my surprise, I added, "Good friends." Not wanting to continue with that line of conversation, I quickly asked, "Would you like to hear something else?"

"Something lively," the woman responded. She suggested a couple of songs I'd never heard of, but I finally thought of one she'd know.

"How about this one?" I played the first few notes of "California Here I Come" before Mitch came in with the words. The woman helped, too, keeping time with one of her hands.

I was looking down at the keys when I noticed that the tapping had stopped. A split second later the woman crumpled to the floor.

Both Mitch and I were frozen in shock for a moment. Then he quickly rose from the piano bench and ran toward the door. "I'll get help," he called.

By this point a few of the lounge visitors had joined me at the woman's side. I was scared and tried with all my might to keep from crying. I'd never seen someone collapse before, and I didn't know what to do. I hoped the doctors got there soon.

The woman's eyes were open, and she seemed to be trying to say something, but she couldn't talk or move. A man told me to get out of the way, but I felt I had to do something, so I held her hand in my palm and stroked it gently with my other hand. "Don't worry, you're going to be OK," I kept telling her.

Less than a minute later Mitch ran back in. Following him closely was a woman doctor and a nurse, who was wheeling in a cart full of medicine and some monitoring equipment. "Let us in," the doctor ordered. I backed away, but my eyes stayed glued to the old woman.

I let Mitch hold me as we walked back to my room. I was shaken by the experience, and right then I really needed him.

Mitch sat down on the bed with me. "Are you OK?" he asked.

I nodded my head. "I'll be all right," I said. "What if she dies, Mitch?"

"The doctor's there. I'm sure she's doing everything she can."

"I know, but I'm scared. I mean, what if my playing brought on her collapse or something?"

Mitch gently patted my arm, comforting me the way I'd comforted the woman. "You can't think like that. Believe me, I know."

"But you don't play—" I stopped as I looked up at his caring eyes, now filled with sadness. "What's wrong, Mitch?"

"My father died three years ago. He'd been sick for a long time before that, and he'd spent a lot of time in the hospital. I was nine the first time he went in. I'll never forget it. The day before, I'd been out playing with my friends and accidentally threw a baseball through the garage window. He bawled me out plenty for that, and then the next thing I knew he was in the hospital. He was there for three weeks. For a long time I thought I'd put him there. I thought that if I hadn't broken that window, he never would have gotten sick. But, of course, it wasn't true. Just like what happened with that woman. Some things just happen."

My eyes had begun to fill with tears. "Oh, Mitch, I'm so sorry. I didn't know."

"Hey, it's OK. Really. I'm fine." Mitch put up a good front, but I sensed the pain he was feeling.

I wrapped an arm around his back. "It must have been so hard for you."

He put his arm around me and pulled me close, so that my head was nestled on his shoulder. "It was hard on all of us, but on my mom more than anyone else. I don't know how she did it—going to work, taking care of Dad and us. But she managed. It showed me I could, too. I hope you get a chance to meet her someday. I think you'd like her."

"I'd like to," I said.

"Does that mean you meant what you told that woman?"

"What's that?"

"That we're *good* friends?"

I smiled. "I guess it does."

For a long time after that, we sat there saying nothing, just holding each other—in friendship.

Chapter Seven

"How about one of your rousing cheers, Gretchen!" Sean said, bursting into my room that evening. He was bubbling over with excitement, which made me feel awful that I wasn't in as glowing a mood.

"What am I supposed to be cheering about?" I asked, sitting up.

Sean plopped down on the bed. "You're looking at the Brimley most valuable player of the game."

"Hey, Sean, that's terrific!" I cried. I leaned over to give him a big hug. I moved a little too fast, though, and the pain made me wince.

"You OK?" he asked.

I managed a smile. "I'll be all right," I said, lying back on the pillows. "Gee, it's great to see you."

"Hey, I've missed you, too," he said. "So what have you been doing to keep busy?"

"Well." I thought for a moment. "I discovered the lounge. There's a piano there."

"Knowing you, you've probably been playing lots of tunes to keep the old folks happy." Sean began playing an imaginary piano, bopping his head around like a human metronome.

But I didn't laugh. His words reminded me of Mrs. DaSilva. That was the name of the woman from the lounge. I found that out after dinner when a nurse came in to give me my medication.

Sean stopped when he saw I wasn't reacting. "I thought I was being funny, but I see I've got a tough audience."

"Something bad happened today."

"Want to tell me about it?"

"I was playing the piano for an old woman. She collapsed right in the middle of a song."

"Couldn't stand your playing, huh," he quipped.

I wasn't in the mood to see the humor. "It's not funny, Sean. She almost died."

"Is she going to be all right?"

"The nurse says she's 'stable,' but I won't believe it till I see for myself. And they're not letting her have any visitors right now."

"You can't do anything about the situation now, so why worry?"

"I suppose you're right." Trying to lighten

the conversation, I added, "You know, I'm not sure I should leave this hospital so soon. I mean, look what happened. I leave you alone, and you go off and get most valuable player."

"Your absence had nothing to do with it. I just got lucky."

"Come on, Sean. You know that's not true."

He played around with the blanket. "Well, I was on a roll this week. Last night I scored twenty-eight points against Jefferson. My best ever! And I had ten rebounds!"

"All right!" I waved my fist in the air.

"You should have seen it, Gretch," he went on. "We were closing in on halftime. The score was close—thirty-eight to thirty-six—and we were supposed to beat Jefferson easily. So I got mad and really went to town. I grabbed a rebound and threw it across court to Jeremy, who sunk the basket. Then I batted the ball away from one of their guys and dunked it—all in the space of about five seconds. By halftime we were leading by five—and those Jeff guys knew something had happened. But it was in the second half that I scored most of my points. We really blew them away!"

"My hero," I exclaimed. It was great to see Sean so happy, so proud of himself.

There was only one thing wrong. I wasn't feeling as happy for him as I knew I should.

* * *

Mitch burst into my room the following day. "Come on, Gretchen, I've got a surprise for you."

I had no idea what was on his mind, but he practically pulled me out of bed. "What's the hurry?"

"Just wait and see," he said, dragging me to the lounge. "Look who's here!" he announced.

He pointed to Mrs. DaSilva, who was sitting in a wheelchair next to the window reading a book. "See, she's all right."

"I know," I said.

"I wanted to surprise you," he said with disappointment.

"I stopped in to see her this morning, as soon as one of the nurses said I could," I explained. "She told me she'd just had a bad reaction to one of the pills they'd given her."

"I should have realized you'd know by now. After all, you were here all day, and I was in school."

"How is it out in the real world?"

"Look." He pushed up his sweater to show me his cast, now covered almost entirely with doodles, pictures, and signatures. "A couple of my friends told me I should have broken my leg. It would have given them a bigger cast to work on."

"Nice friends you've got there," I said.

Mrs. DaSilva noticed us then and waved us over. "Would you play something for me, dear?"

I played several songs before Mrs. DaSilva said she felt tired and wanted to go back to her room for a rest. She left, and Mitch and I were alone in the room. We moved from the piano bench to a couch.

"She's a nice woman," Mitch said.

"I know," I replied quietly. "You know, it's funny how you get to know people in the hospital. I'd never have met Mrs. DaSilva if I hadn't gotten sick. And Rachel. I'd never tell her this, but when she first told me she was getting a tummy tuck, I wanted to laugh. I couldn't believe anyone would be crazy enough to do such a thing. But the more we talked, the more I realized that she was really suffering. She hated her body so much that she'd undergo surgery to change it. Now I also have more sympathy for some of the overweight girls at school who are forever dieting. It must be awfully hard for them."

"It's got to be hard for you, too—being stuck here while Sean and your friends are out having fun."

"It's not so bad. And knowing you has made the hospital much more bearable." Impulsively, I kissed him gently on the cheek. Without a word, he kissed me back, this time on the lips. It felt warm and soft and gentle, all the things a kiss should be. As we broke apart, I looked up and was shocked to see Sean's steely hazel eyes looking down at me.

"Uh, hi, there," I said with a gulp. Turning away from Mitch, I went on, "Nice to see you, Sean."

"Is it?" he rasped. "I went to your room to see you, and you weren't there. I had no idea where you'd gone."

"I told you Dr. Benard wanted me to get some exercise," I said. "Mitch was kind enough to walk me down here."

"Well, I can take over now," Sean said, looking at Mitch pointedly.

"I can see I'd better be going." Mitch stood up and extended his hand to Sean. "Nice to meet you. I've heard lots of good things about you from Gretchen. You've got a fine girlfriend, Sean. Take good care of her."

Sean didn't take his hand. He didn't say anything. He just stood there, seething and watching Mitch head toward the door.

Alone with Sean, I didn't know what to say. I walked over to the piano. "Uh, want to play?" I asked, tinkling the piano keys.

Sean just glared at me. "What's going on here?" he demanded.

"Uh, not here," I said, looking around. "Let's go back to my room." I started to leave, and Sean grabbed my arm, marching alongside me. Neither one of us said a word. It only took us a couple of minutes to get back, but they felt like the longest two minutes of my life.

Rachel was in the room when we got there, so I closed the gold curtain between our beds to give Sean and me a little privacy. "It's not what you think," I said in a low voice, "Mitch is just a friend."

"Are you always so intimate with friends?" he snapped back.

"Come on, Sean," I challenged. "Haven't you ever felt grateful to someone? Mitch has been very kind to me."

"And just what has he done? How much time have you been spending with him, anyway?"

"He's come by every day."

"*Every* day?" Sean exclaimed. "Boy, you sure don't waste any time, do you, Gretchen?"

"What's that supposed to mean?"

"I can't be here all the time, so you go and find someone who can."

I shook my head in amazement. "I can't

believe you think I'd do that. You know how much I care about you, Sean."

"Then how come you didn't tell me about Mitch sooner?"

"Maybe because I had a hunch you wouldn't understand."

"What wouldn't I understand? A kiss is a kiss. It's as plain as night and day."

"I was right. You don't understand. You're overreacting."

"No, I'm not. You've betrayed me, Gretchen."

I was seeing a side of Sean I'd never seen before—and I didn't like it. "It was just one little kiss. I'd hardly call that a betrayal."

He paced back and forth along the side of the bed. "It's not just the kiss, it's last night, too. At the time it didn't click, but there was something different about you. You seemed—distracted."

"I was upset about Mrs. DaSilva," I explained. "By the way, she's going to be all right."

"I don't care about her. I care about us—or what I thought was us."

"What's that supposed to mean?"

"When I asked you to go with me, I expected you to stay loyal to me. But now I don't know that I can trust you to do that anymore, Gretchen."

"Come on, Sean, you've got to believe me. I'm not interested in Mitch."

"I don't have to do anything," he said coldly. "Goodbye."

"Will I see you tomorrow?"

"Don't expect me to come back ever."

Just like that he stormed out, practically ripping the curtain off the rings as he pulled it aside. I looked over at Rachel, who was looking at me curiously, and shrugged. I didn't want to talk about it—not with her, not with anyone. Instead, I grabbed Pooh, and hugging him, I cried until I fell asleep.

Chapter Eight

Early the following morning Melinda called me. "What happened last night?" she asked. "Sean came home in a fit and wouldn't speak to anyone. This morning he suggested I cancel your party, and when I told him I wouldn't, he said he'd make plans to stay away from the house all night. Gretchen, what's going on?"

"Your brother has a vivid imagination, that's what," I said flatly. "Remember that guy you met when you came to see me? Well, we've become friends over the past few days. Just friends, nothing more. But Sean has us practically married. I tried to tell him, but he wouldn't believe me."

"Yeah, that sounds like Sean," Melinda agreed.

"Do you think he'll change his mind? I don't want to lose him."

"I don't want you to, either. But I think you

already have. You know how stubborn Sean is."

"That's not exactly what I wanted to hear. Oh, by the way, I found out last night that I'm getting out of here today at noon."

"Great!" Melinda said excitedly. "Should I organize a party for tomorrow night? Or would you rather not have it because of Sean?"

"I think I'm going to need all the cheering up I can get. Sunday night would be fine. I'm not up to staying out late, though."

"That's OK," Melinda said. "My parents wouldn't let me have a late-night party when we have school the next day, anyway."

After I got off the phone, I sank back into my depression. Sean and I were through. The words sounded so unreal. How could it be over just like that? I thought of Mitch, of sitting down with him and pouring out my troubles. He'd know what to say, he'd come up with the words that would make me feel better.

But after what happened in the lounge, I doubted he'd be stopping by anymore. The thought of not seeing Mitch again both upset and relieved me. I mean, there I was, broken-hearted about losing the boy of my dreams, and at the same time I was brooding about not seeing a boy who had been a stranger to me a week before.

It was too much to cope with, so I tried to put both boys out of my mind.

I must have drifted off to sleep for a few minutes because Ms. Halstead woke me up when she came in. "Sorry to get you up," she said, but her voice indicated very little sympathy. "But it's time for you to start getting ready to check out. Your parents will be here in a while."

"What time is it?" I mumbled. I was too groggy to consult the watch tucked away in my bedside table drawer.

"A little after ten."

In spite of my resolve, I still had boys on the brain. But I was shocked that I'd just thought of Mitch, not Sean. The truth was I wanted to see Mitch more than I wanted to see Sean. Sometime in the past few days my feelings for Mitch had changed. I was afraid he wouldn't know where to find me after I'd left. "I have to admit, Gretchen, after you had that relapse, I expected you to take a long time to recover. But you've snapped back very fast. Call me if you need any help getting ready."

She left the room. Desperately, I kept glancing at the door, hoping Mitch would walk in.

He didn't know I'd be leaving, and if he didn't come now, I'd never see him again!

After I was dressed, I became more and more restless. Realizing I'd drive myself insane if I stayed in my room, I decided to stop by the lounge. At least there I could play the piano. Maybe Mrs. DaSilva would be there, too, or someone else I could talk with. Quickly I scribbled a note to my parents indicating where I was going, then left it on my pillow.

I opened the door to the lounge. Standing by the window, much as he had been the day before, was Mitch. "What are *you* doing here?" I cried out.

Several of the patients sitting nearby turned around to look at me, but they returned to their activities when they realized I wasn't speaking to them.

Mitch turned around, too, and looked at me shyly. His eyes darted from me to the floor. "I wasn't sure you'd want to see me."

"That's not true," I protested, walking over to him. Mitch pointed to an empty sofa, and we both sat down.

"I've been in here wondering if I should come in to see you again or whether I'd be wasting my time."

"It's a good thing you didn't leave," I said. "I have something to tell you. They're springing me from this place in an hour. I'm going home! Doctor Benard told me last night after you left."

"That's great!" Mitch smiled.

"Of course, I'm not going to be able to go back to school just yet. They want me to build up my strength. But it'll be wonderful to be in my own room again."

"Let me see if I can guess what your room looks like. I'll bet you've got a big white bed with one of those canopies and a stereo and TV and lots of bookshelves and a big, thick carpet."

I smiled. "The bed is bleached oak, and I took the canopy off a few years ago, but you're right about the rest. How'd you know?"

"Just a hunch," he said. "If I were designing a room for you, that's the type of stuff I'd put in it."

"Could you add a gym and a sauna?" I asked hopefully. "I pleaded with my dad to buy us a Nautilus machine, but he said, 'No way.' "

"I'd get it for you if I could." He sighed. Turning more serious, Mitch looked at me. "I'm going to miss you, Gretchen."

"Just because I'm leaving the hospital doesn't mean I'm walking out of your life."

"You mean you'd still like to see me? What about Sean?"

"We broke up," I said, still finding the words hard to say.

"But why?"

"He couldn't deal with seeing us together yesterday. I don't know, maybe he was just smarter than I was and saw something there that I didn't. I really thought you and I were nothing more than friends. But today I wondered what would happen if I didn't see you again. I couldn't bear it," I said.

"You don't know how much I've wanted to hear you say that. See, I have a confession to make. I've cared for you all along." Mitch put his good arm around me and pulled me close.

Then he touched his lips to mine. I loved the feel of his arm around me. I returned his kiss with an intensity I'd never felt when I was kissing Sean. Mitch was different. I couldn't explain how or why. All I knew was that I liked being with him and wanted to see him again.

"When can I see you again?" Mitch asked.

"I've got a great idea. Melinda is having a party for me tomorrow night. I'd like you to come."

"Are you going to be up for a party so soon?"

"I won't be doing any dancing, that's for sure. And it won't be a late night. But I'm up to seeing my friends. It should be fun."

"Will Sean be there?"

"No. All my other friends will be, though. I'd like you to meet them. Got some paper? I'll give you her address."

"Here." He fished out a bus transfer from his pocket and handed it to me. Quickly I scribbled down Melinda's address.

"Hmm," he said, looking at the address. "Must be a pretty fancy house."

"Oh, it's not really that special," I said. "Not like your architectural dream house."

"OK, I'll be there," Mitch said and smiled.

Chapter Nine

Melinda was sitting across from me in our living room later that day, telling me about the party. "Everything's all set. I've told the entire gang to be at my place tomorrow night at seven sharp!"

"I'm so excited. I wouldn't miss it for anything," I said.

"You'd better not. What kind of party would it be if the guest of honor didn't show up? But I have to admit I'm a little concerned. I haven't seen you budge out of that chair since I got here."

"Give me a break. I've just had my appendix out," I said. I squirmed into an even more comfortable position in the big leather chair. My legs were resting on the matching black ottoman. Peaches, my dog, was sleeping peacefully at my feet. "I'm just reacquainting myself with the comforts of home."

Melinda sighed. "I guess if I'd been in a hospital for a week, I'd do the same thing—" she said and paused. "I'm sorry I didn't come and visit you more," she continued. "But I don't like hospitals. They remind me of when my grandfather died."

"I'll say this much—it *is* like being in a different world. High school and everything else seemed so foreign there, almost as if they didn't exist. Now that I'm home, though, it's almost as if I was never gone."

"By tomorrow night you're going to have forgotten all about that place," Melinda said. "Everybody's going to want to fill you in on what you've missed—which probably isn't much, actually."

I thought it was very tactful of her not to mention Sean. I knew Melinda was upset about our breakup, and I was glad she didn't press the issue.

"Something wrong?" Melinda asked.

"Oh, no," I said, lying. "I was just wondering what I'm going to wear to the party. I still can't wear anything tight fitting."

Melinda looked at me thoughtfully for a moment. "What about your pink and white T-shirt dress?" she suggested. "It's loose and casual—and looks terrific on you."

"Yeah. That's a good idea," I said. "Uh, by

the way, Melinda, I invited someone to the party."

"Not that guy I saw you with at the hospital?" Melinda's dark brown eyebrows shot up accusingly.

"Well, yes. And his name is Mitch."

"Was Sean right? Is anything going on between you two?"

I shrugged. "There wasn't. Like I told you before, we were just two hospital patients trying to help each other pass the time. But I'm not going out with Sean anymore, I may want to see more of Mitch. He's really awfully nice. Anyway, I thought the party would be a good place for him to meet everyone."

"I see," Melinda said. "In that case, I suppose it'll be all right."

I understood her need to reserve judgment on Mitch. She'd wanted to see Sean and me together almost as long as I had. But I had a hunch she'd like Mitch once she got to know him. All it would take was a little time.

Melinda's house was built for partying. A large family room was separate from the rest of their sprawling house. The room even had its own entrance from the back, so Melinda's parents wouldn't be disturbed by the comings and goings.

Melinda had done a terrific job getting the place set up for the party. The track lights in the middle of the room were turned down low, accenting the fire burning in the white brick fireplace. The refrigerator was packed with soda, and there were bowls of popcorn, chips, and other munchies. Some pizzas were ready to warm in the oven. Over in a corner the TV was set on the video channel, and music was blasting out of the speakers at either end of the room.

Melinda had insisted on my not doing anything to help, but I came early anyway. My dad dropped me off since I was still in no condition to drive. "I feel like a queen," I told her from my perch on her gray corduroy sofa. "Are you sure there's nothing I can do?"

"Just wait for the guests to arrive," Melinda called brightly from the bar where she was cramming even more soda cans into the refrigerator.

"Well, here's one of them."

Two large paper bags partially covered Sean's face as he walked into the room. "I knew you'd forget about the ice, Melinda, so I went out and got some for you."

I looked at him in shock and then turned to Melinda. She appeared to be equally surprised. "I think this ought to be enough, don't you?" he continued. Quickly he set the bags down and came over to sit by me, putting his arms around me.

"Ooh," I shouted, inching away. "Your hands are freezing!"

"Hey, is that any way to greet me?"

"Sorry," I said, moving back. "I wasn't expecting such a chilly greeting. In fact, I wasn't expecting to see you at all."

"I've been a real fool, Gretchen," he said seriously. "I shouldn't have blown up like I did the other night. You were so right. I was an idiot, overreacting like I did. And I've been miserable ever since. Can you forgive me?"

"But—but—" I couldn't get my mouth to work. *What about Mitch?* I thought.

"You don't have to say it," he went on. "I know this must sound strange after what I said the other night. But, Gretch, I haven't been able to get you out of my mind. I thought about how good things were for us before you went to the hospital. Maybe I just don't understand how lonely it can get in a hospital. I should have taken your word that that guy meant nothing to you."

"Oh, Sean," I cried. Why couldn't he have said that before? He was saying everything I wanted to hear, and sitting on that sofa next to him, where I'd sat with him so many times before, everything felt so right.

But in no time at all Mitch would be there. It was too late to tell him not to come. And even if I could still catch him, I had no idea what I'd tell him.

"So what do you say, Gretchen? Can we give it another try?"

What could I say? I cared so much for Sean. "I'm glad you changed your mind," I said finally.

I should have told him right then that Mitch was coming, but the timing wasn't right. I mean, what could I have said, "Sean, I just want you to know that the guy you think means nothing to me is coming over tonight"? If I did, I was sure he'd walk right out of the house, and I didn't want to risk that.

Besides, just because Sean had had a change of heart didn't mean I didn't want to see Mitch. I'd had daydreams about how the party would go, how Mitch would make a big hit with my friends, how much fun it'd be to finally spend some time with him out of the hospital. Those daydreams hadn't fizzled. The truth was I cared about them both.

The only thing I could do was try to spend time with both of them. It wouldn't be the first time a girl had had two boyfriends. I could be like the heroine from one of those old screwball, black-and-white comedies. Maybe I'd be able to pull it off and not lose either Sean or Mitch.

But, of course, it didn't work out that way at all.

Mitch hadn't even arrived before I knew I was in for a tough evening. I told some friends how Mitch had saved me from myself when I had gone in search of the granola bar, concluding with "I don't know what would have happened to me if Mitch hadn't been there." Sean happened to catch that last line and gave me a funny look. I smiled at him, to reassure him that things between us were fine. I don't know why I did it, because I knew things *weren't* fine.

Mitch walked in a few minutes after that, looking fantastic. His hair was brushed back, and the all-black outfit he wore made him stand out among my more conservatively dressed friends. Seeing him made me realize just how much I'd missed him.

I caught his eye, and he smiled, looking relieved to have found a familiar face. I didn't think Mitch would feel awkward in a crowd, but I suppose even the most self-assured person gets nervous in a roomful of strangers.

I wanted to run up to him, but Sean was

nearby, and I didn't want him to see us. Mitch started to approach me but fortunately was waylaid near the edge of the sofa by Betsy. "You must be Mitch," she said, loud enough for half the world to hear. "Gretchen's told me so much about you." She was moving in on him. But I realized that as far as Betsy knew, he was fair game.

I was pleased that Mitch was kind enough not to ignore her. "And who are you?" he asked in his friendly way.

"My name's Betsy. We almost met once at the hospital. How's your arm feeling?"

Mitch answered politely, but he looked as though he wanted to be rescued. Forcing myself off the sofa, I made my way over to them. "Hi, Mitch. I see you've met one of my friends," I said brightly.

"Yes," he said. But his eyes seemed to be pleading with me to find a place where we could be alone.

"Betsy, could you excuse us for a moment? I want to show Mitch around, make him feel at home."

"Oh, I can do that," she offered.

"No, he's my guest," I insisted.

Betsy walked away, leaving us alone. Mitch began to pull me close, but I backed away. It didn't seem right to be so affectionate with him in Sean's house. "Hey, what's wrong?" he asked. "Aren't you glad to see me?"

I didn't really know what to say to him. Everything was different now. "Sure I am," I said.

"You're not acting it."

"Well, something's come up." Mitch followed my glance to where Sean was pouring sodas for his friends.

"What's he doing here?" His voice was harsher than I'd ever heard it before. "You told me he wouldn't be around."

"Believe me, I was just as surprised as you are."

"Didn't you tell Sean about us?" Mitch asked.

"Well, not exactly—"

"What are you waiting for?" Mitch tried to draw me closer to him.

"Not now!" I hissed. "Someone could see us."

"That didn't seem to bother you in the hospital." Mitch began to move closer again, and once more I resisted.

"That was different," I said. "All these people weren't around then."

"You mean Sean." The snarl returned to Mitch's voice.

But no sooner were the words out than Sean

came gliding to my side. "I saw you get up from the sofa, and I got worried," he said. Then he looked directly at Mitch. "What are you doing here?"

"Gretchen invited me."

"Well, you're not welcome in my house. If you know what's good for you, you'll leave."

"No, I won't," Mitch declared.

Sean looked as if he were ready to punch Mitch, and I stepped between them. "Sean, can I see you a minute?" I pulled him over to the wall next to the stereo. "Listen, I don't want you to make a scene."

Sean's face was flushed with anger. "Well, what's he doing here?"

"Like he told you, I invited him." Before Sean could get mad at me, I continued, "Don't get angry. Why shouldn't I have invited him? You'd made it perfectly clear to me that we were through. And I didn't want to come to this party and mope around all night. So I asked Mitch to come. We were just friends in the hospital. You've got to believe that."

Sean looked as if he was going to say something but then thought better of it. "And now?"

I clasped his hands and faced him squarely. "Give me a few minutes alone with Mitch. Then I'll be back."

"For the rest of the party?" he demanded. "If the answer is no, Gretchen, don't think about coming back at all."

I didn't like being put on the spot like that, but then again, I had asked for it. I thought about Sean and wondered if I wanted to throw away all the fun and good times we'd had. Then I looked at Mitch, who was standing with his back pressed against the sliding glass door, looking abandoned. It would be hard, but I knew what I had to do.

"For the rest of the party," I told Sean.

Believe me, it wasn't easy for me as I took Mitch's arm and led him to the nearest unoccupied corner. "I feel just awful about this," I began.

Mitch snickered. "I understand. You didn't know Sean was going to be here."

"Oh, Mitch, you're only making this harder." I took a deep breath to try to steady myself. "Sean asked me to go with him again—and I said yes."

His smile faded. "Just like that?"

I looked down at the gray tweed carpet beneath my feet. Anything was easier than having to look Mitch in the face. "I know how I'm hurting you, and I feel awful about it. I really like you, Mitch—"

"Well, this is some way to show it."

"Please, let me explain." I opened the glass door. "Let's go outside."

He followed me onto the Flanderses' patio. We began to walk along the concrete path that bordered the swimming pool and Mrs. Flanders's flower garden. "See, Mitch, I like you, but Sean is making me make a choice. And the two of us—we've got a history. I've known Sean almost all my life. We were having a great time together till I got sick, and now that I'm back home, well, it feels right to be with him again. It's for the best."

"What about what happened with us?"

"I'm sorry, Mitch. You really helped me get through an awful time. But that was in the hospital, and I think that everything that happened between us might have been because we were in a different world, cut off from our normal lives."

"I thought you really cared."

"I do care. What I'm trying to say is that when people only know each other under special circumstances, sometimes they appear to be different from what they are in the regular world. That's what happened with us. Could we try to be friends still?"

Mitch gave me kind of a half smirk. "Yeah, friends," he said bitterly. "I see it now. When a girl gets back into surroundings like these, it's only natural that she's not going to want to hang out with a guy like me. I should have seen it coming." He started to walk toward the front of the house, and I followed after him.

"I wish things could have been different," I called out to him.

"Me, too," he said. He reached the gate to the street. "I guess I'd better be going. Goodbye, Gretchen."

"Goodbye, Mitch." My tear-filled eyes were blurring my view of him. Quickly I wiped them away and walked back to the party.

Chapter Ten

During the next few days most of my daytime hours were spent catching up on schoolwork. Fortunately I hadn't missed all that much. And since school had always come fairly easily to me, the work was more time consuming than difficult. I did enjoy spending time on my genetics report. And thanks to our computer, I was able to access some research materials from our subscription data source.

One day I was particularly excited when I found new research studies that linked specific chromosomes with diabetes. The first thing I told Sean when he called that night was about the chromosomes.

"Terrific," Sean said. But I could tell he wasn't really interested.

"Don't you understand what this means? It could lead to a cure. It's another step in figuring out what really makes us what we are. Someday, through genetic engineering, scientists will be able to prevent other problems, too, like Down's syndrome and hemophilia."

"Call me when they do," Sean said flippantly. "Gretchen, you'll never believe what Coach Reiner did at basketball practice." He didn't wait for a reply. "A couple of us guys were clowning around—nothing really bad—and he really got steamed. He made everyone shoot foul shots for an hour!"

"Knowing Reiner, he was probably upset about your losing the last game."

"Yeah, but we were working hard before that. Besides, goofing off is half the fun."

"Speaking of goofing off, Mom says I can go out this weekend," I announced, changing the subject to something more relevant to the two of us. "I convinced her that I'm ready to rejoin the world. And since I'll be going back to school on Monday, she really couldn't say no."

"That's the best news I've heard," Sean said. "Want to see a movie?"

"Sure. I heard that new Meryl Streep movie's supposed to be pretty good."

"Naw, too heavy for me," Sean said. "Let's go to the new horror flick at the Movieplex."

"Do we have to?" I groaned.

"What's the matter?"

"I don't know." I hated horror movies.

"I've been waiting till you got better just so I could take you to this new movie."

"Really? Maybe I'll give it a try then."

The movie was worse than I thought it would be. I couldn't believe that a nice, intelligent guy like Sean would find all that violence appealing. Half the time I wouldn't even look at the screen. Near the end I was snapped to attention when a huge explosion shattered my eardrums.

"Now, wasn't that a terrific film?" Sean asked as we were walking out.

"Sure," I said agreeably.

"All that excitement's got me hungry. Let's go to the Cheshire Cat."

"Couldn't we go to Tito's? I've been dying for a chili burrito for days."

Sean wrinkled his nose. "You sure you can eat that stuff?"

"I can eat anything I want now."

"But the whole gang's going to be at the Cat."

Sean was really upsetting me. He seemed happy enough to be with me, but he didn't want to take my feelings into consideration when he made plans. It wasn't intentional on his part. I think he just assumed that I'd naturally want to do the things he did. His asking me was done as a sort of courtesy more than anything else.

But I didn't make a big deal over it. I really didn't mind going to the Cheshire Cat. Located across the street from our school, it was a popular hangout. As soon as we walked in, Melinda got up and waved at us to join her at one of the booths in the back. Betsy, Clare, Mike, and a couple of other kids from school were already there. I sat down next to Betsy.

"So how was the movie?" Melinda asked.

"Fantastic!" Sean immediately started retelling the entire story of the movie.

"I've heard this one," I said, squirming out of the seat again. "I'll be in the ladies' room," I whispered to Betsy. She didn't seem interested in the plot either.

I'd always liked the Cheshire Cat's bathroom. The walls are painted a nice warm pink, and the big mirror that stretches across the triple sink counter is lined with light bulbs. The lighting is very flattering. Standing before the mirror, I inspected my makeup, viewing with distress the little pimple that had appeared on my chin. Trying to distract myself from the unsightly spot, I took out my brush and began pulling it through my hair.

Betsy walked in and hopped up on the coun-

a cheeseburger and fries on the table in front of me. "Is this for me?" I asked Sean.

"I ordered for you while you were gone," Sean said. An identical order was facing him.

It wasn't what I would have ordered, but I obligingly picked up the burger and began eating. I didn't feel up to arguing that evening.

Chapter Eleven

The following Monday there was a large brown envelope waiting for me when I got home from school.

I opened it carefully, and when I saw what was inside, my heart fell. It was the sketch Mitch had drawn of me in the hospital. No note. No explanation.

Clutching the drawing to my chest, I ran to my room and slammed the door before falling on my bed and crying uncontrollably. There was no doubt in my mind that Mitch had sent this back to me because he wanted nothing more to do with me. I suppose it was silly of me to think we could have continued to be "friends."

I wished I could have taken the environment we'd created in the hospital and transferred it into the real world. But I knew, despite my sadness, that I belonged with Sean. "Isn't that right, Pooh?" I looked at the bear, now back in his usual spot on my bookcase.

As I hid the picture in the back of my closet, I realized that I still cared a lot for Mitch. It made me very sad to realize that he had no desire ever to see me again.

"OK, gang, let's go! Once around the track. Feet up! Get moving!"

I sat in the bleachers on Thursday as Coach Nayoka barked her orders. Because I still was recovering, I was excused from PE. Still, I was expected to show up for class. I used the period to try to catch up on what I'd missed at school. History was difficult because we were studying the Revolutionary War, and I was having a hard time getting all those generals and battles straight.

During a break I looked wistfully at my classmates. I wanted to be out there with them. Running was one of my passions; it's a great way to clear the brain.

But instead I had plenty of time to think, and I was starting to believe I was going a little batty. Getting that picture back from Mitch had started me thinking about him a lot. I realized I hadn't stopped caring about him at all. Remembering his concern and his thoughtfulness, I'd wanted to rush to the nearest phone and call him. But I never did because I'd remember the last time I saw him. He had looked so hopeless and disappointed in me. I didn't think I could stand the hurt of having him reject me. I kept trying to convince myself that it was better to keep things as they were.

On Saturday I made a picnic lunch, which Sean and I took to my favorite spot in Angeles National Forest.

"Isn't this beautiful?" I asked him, staring at the tall pine and spruce trees that formed a green curtain around us.

"Trees are trees," he answered flatly. "What's really beautiful is right here, next to me." With that he took me in his arms and kissed me.

Sean pulled away from me, and I realized sadly that I was relieved. "I'm hungry. What's to eat?" he asked.

I flipped open the picnic basket. "Let's see. Some fried chicken, cole slaw, potato chips—" I said as I took the food containers out.

"I'll have some chicken," Sean said. I couldn't help but wonder if he was always this self-absorbed.

I opened the plastic tub, removed the chicken pieces, and put them on a paper plate. He grabbed a couple of sodas from the Styrofoam cooler.

"You going to be cheering for me at the Taft game?" he asked, biting into a chicken leg.

"When is it?" I asked.

"You don't know? They're our biggest rivals!"

To Sean, forgetting the basketball schedule was an unpardonable sin. "Well, since I'm not cheering now, it's hard for me to remember who we play when."

"Friday night. You'll be there, won't you?"

"Sure," I said, figuring I could make room for the game.

"Wait till you see what we've got planned," Sean said excitedly. "Coach Reiner made us learn a whole new zone defense just for the Taft game. They're really going to be surprised. Here's how it works. . . ."

To be fair to Sean, basketball has always been his greatest love. It was natural that he'd want to share it with me. But he'd told me about this game plan the night before, and I got bored hearing about it again. As he talked, I concentrated more on my food than I did on him, and he noticed. "What's wrong?" he asked.

"Oh, nothing," I lied.

Sean put down his plate and stared at me.

"Come on, Gretch, I can tell something's bothering you. What is it?"

More than anything, I wanted things between us to be the way they were. I wanted to be able to talk to Sean the way I'd been able to talk to Mitch. Testing the waters, I ventured, "Do you think we could talk about something other than basketball?"

"What else is there?" he asked.

"Look around us, Sean. Don't you ever get amazed at the beauty around us? Don't you ever think about how magnificent it is?"

"I thought we came here to spend some time together, not look at trees," he said, nuzzling the back of my neck.

"That's not what I meant."

"What is it then?"

"Never mind, you wouldn't understand," I said in a resigned voice. "Do you want to hear how I'm doing on my genetics report?"

"You know that stuff bores me," he said. "What about Mrs. Rossner? Did I tell you about what happened yesterday?"

I nodded.

The silence between us was overwhelming, so I looked at a squirrel scurrying for nuts. Sean just reached over and helped himself to another piece of chicken.

Chapter Twelve

The following morning I answered the door bell and was shocked to see Sean standing there. "What are you doing up so early?"

"We're all going to the desert for the day. How soon can you be ready?" He surveyed my outfit. "Put something decent on, OK? Jim's waiting in the van." He walked into the house and into the kitchen where my parents were sitting at the table. "Hi, Mr. and Mrs. Diamond. I'm taking Gretchen out to the desert. But don't worry, I'll have her back by dinner time."

He didn't even ask me if I wanted to go with him. I fumed silently.

"She could use the fresh air," my mother said pleasantly. She adored Sean.

"But I have an English paper to write," I protested, more against his method than out of any desire to waste my day on homework.

"You can do it on the way out there," Sean said.

"What are we going out there for, anyway?"

"Bike riding. Jim knows this great place to rent them. It'll be great."

I looked at him in amazement. "I can't go bike riding. I'm recovering from appendicitis."

"Come on. You'll be fine."

"Sean, there's a tremendous difference between walking in a park and riding a three-wheeled motorcycle. Being on one of those is like riding a jackhammer."

Sean looked at me sheepishly. "I should have thought of that. Well, why don't you come along anyway? At least we can be together for the ride there."

"I have a better idea. If you want to spend the day with me, we can stay here. We can go for a ride in Baby and talk."

"No, I want to go biking," he said. "Anyway, the guys are waiting outside. Sure you don't want to come?"

I shook my head. "It wouldn't be much fun."

"In that case, I'll see you tomorrow in school."

"Probably not. I've got to leave early for my doctor's appointment. I'm going to miss study hall."

"Well, I'll be busy with practice after school. I'll give you a call tonight."

But he didn't call—and I didn't stay up all night worrying about it either. Things between us had definitely changed since my return from the hospital. It was too late to pretend otherwise.

The only thing was—I didn't know if I had the guts to do anything about it.

"You're doing great," Dr. Benard said to me when I went back for my check-up. "The scar is healing nicely, and you seem to have recovered well from the operation. We'll have you back in your cheerleading uniform in no time at all."

"How soon?" I asked eagerly.

"Just another couple of weeks. In fact, you can start doing light workouts now."

"Does that mean I'll be able to go out for track this spring?"

Dr. Benard smiled. "Well, don't order your uniform yet. But if you keep up this recovery, you'll be running laps around all of us."

"Outstanding," I said.

"Don't get carried away. No daredevil acts yet, understand?"

"Don't worry. I promise to take it easy."

It was a quarter to four when I left the

doctor's office. The building he was in was right next to the hospital complex, so I walked across the bridge between the two buildings and entered the main waiting room. Feeling hungry, I took the elevator down to the cafeteria. As I stood before the vending machines, I thought about the first time I'd been there. Looking around, I almost expected to see Mitch come to save the day for me. He didn't.

I pushed the elevator button for the fourth floor, hoping that Mitch would be there visiting the patients. It wasn't that farfetched a notion, considering how much he enjoyed Mrs. DaSilva. And I also remembered his telling me something about visiting the hospital from time to time to cheer people up.

The elevator stopped at every floor, becoming more and more crowded as we went. As I rode up, I pictured myself meeting Mitch in the patients' lounge.

He'd be singing happily along with the patients. He'd stop singing as soon as he saw me, and he'd rush over and take me in his arms. Then I'd sit down at the piano and play for the entire room. The people in the lounge would be weepy-eyed with happiness. Then we'd say goodbye to everyone and walk down the hall, hand in hand.

I knew my daydream was corny and romantic, but I really wanted to believe it was going to happen that way. I got off the elevator and must have been smiling because Ms. Halstead commented on it as she looked up from her station at the nurses' desk. "You're looking quite chipper, Gretchen. I suppose you're glad to be out of here." She laughed. "What can we do for you today?"

"Just visiting," I commented casually.

"Mrs. DaSilva was discharged last week," she told me.

"I'm glad to hear that," I said, pleased that she remembered. "If you don't mind, I thought I'd take a walk down to the lounge," I said. "Goodbye, Ms. Halstead." After taking a few steps, I turned back to face her. "And thank you for taking care of me while I was here."

She looked pleasantly surprised. "Why, you're welcome!" she said with a smile.

With rising anticipation, I walked down the hall to the lounge. I kept looking for Mitch. My heart started beating faster, and my hands started to get clammy. *Relax! This is no time to get nervous*, I told myself.

Taking a deep breath, I pulled the lounge door open. A few women were sitting on the sofas, talking in low voices, and a man in a wheelchair was looking out the window. Another older, white-haired man had his eyes glued to the aquarium. He looked like a friendly person, so I ambled over to him.

"Hi," I said, sitting on a chair next to him.

"Hi, yourself, young lady," he answered back.

I pointed to the tank. "Those jumbo neons are pretty, aren't they? We used to have an aquarium at home, and they were always my favorites."

The man pointed to an ugly gray fish snooping around the bottom, near the coral-colored gravel. "Those neons may look nice, but they're no good for anything else. Now, these catfish there. They're the important ones. They clean up all the garbage from the tank and make it clean for the other fish."

"I never knew that," I said. "My father always cleaned the tank we had."

"Just something I've observed from watching them," the man said.

"Have you been in the hospital long?"

"About a week now," he said.

"Do you come to the lounge a lot?"

The man nodded. "Not too much else to do here, I'm afraid," he said sadly.

"Have you seen a boy around? He'd be about my age with dark, wavy hair and a cast on his right arm?"

"Sorry, don't think I have. I'd remember,

too. There haven't been many young people in here."

"Thanks," I said, standing up. "Hope you feel better soon." I left the lounge and headed toward the elevator. Before leaving, I went to the nurses' station where Ms. Halstead was going over some charts with another nurse.

"Excuse me," I said when she looked up from the charts.

"Leaving so soon?" she asked.

"Yes, I have to go. But before I do, could I ask you a question?"

"Sure."

"Do you remember a dark-haired guy who used to visit me while I was here? Mitch Gantry? He was hospitalized for part of the time I was here."

She thought a moment before nodding her head. "Yes. What about him?"

"Have you seen him lately? I mean, does he come around here and visit other patients?"

"Why, no," she answered quickly.

"Thanks," I answered weakly.

The news bothered me. It meant that I'd lost the last remaining tie that we had in common. There was very little chance we'd ever run into each other. If I ever wanted to see Mitch again, I'd have to call him. I didn't think I could.

Chapter Thirteen

During the ride back home, I made a decision. As soon as I got there, I raced to the phone.

"Melinda?" I said. "Is Sean there?"

"No, he's not back from basketball practice yet, but he ought to be home soon. What's up?"

"I've got to talk to him. Have him call me as soon as he gets in, OK?"

I hung up, but I was so impatient to talk to him that I couldn't wait for his call. Pulling my jacket back on, I went outside and started walking toward Sean's house. It was a good half mile, but Dr. Benard did say I could use some exercise. Besides, I had to tell Sean before I lost my nerve.

I saw Sean pulling into his driveway as I turned the corner of his block. I shouted as loud as I could, "Hey, Sean, wait for me."

By the time I reached him, he was leaning against his Trans Am, looking so appealing that I began to have doubts about my decision. But I couldn't let feelings of nostalgia prevent me from doing what I knew I had to do.

The walk to his house had left me hot and sweaty. I'm sure I looked like a wreck, but I didn't care. In fact, I felt it was an advantage to look as unattractive as I could. But he, on the other hand, had apparently showered after his practice; his hair was still damp, and he had on the cologne I'd given him for Christmas.

"I didn't expect to see you here," Sean said. "Come to see Melinda?"

"No, I took a chance on your being here. We need to talk," I said.

He must have heard the hurt in my voice. "I missed you in school," he said. "We had fun out in the desert, too. I really wish you'd have come along, at least for the ride."

"It's no fun being an observer," I answered.

"I'm really sorry I didn't think about your not being able to ride. It was stupid of me." Sean shuffled his feet nervously.

"You're right, Sean," I said. "You should have been more considerate of what I needed. I know your heart's in the right place, but it's just not enough. All you care about is what you want."

"I want to be with you," he explained.

"No, Sean," I reasoned. "If you'd wanted to spend the day with me, we could have stayed here and done a million things. But you wanted to go biking, and since I'm your girl you thought it would be fun to have me around. That's different from wanting to be with me."

"I'll make it up to you, Gretchen. Really. I promise," he pleaded.

"It's too late, Sean. This whole thing has made me see how one-sided our relationship's been. I've always adored you, and because of that I've put up with a lot of things from you that I wouldn't take from another guy."

"Yeah? Like what?"

"Like taking second place to a car. Like hearing about basketball all day."

"Well, I've put up with a lot of your stuff, too."

"Like what?"

"Like having to listen to you tell about your boring science project."

"It's not boring to me," I said, defending myself.

"And what's the matter with basketball?"

"Nothing. But it's all you seem to live for these days."

"Well, at least I don't go carrying part of my body around in a jar!"

"Time out!" I shouted. "Sean, don't you see what's happening? Let's do ourselves a favor and stop seeing each other while we're still friends."

Sean stood there a moment, his fingers gripping the chrome trim on his car. Then he turned around and fished his gym bag out of the backseat. "OK," he said simply. "Take care, Gretchen." With that he headed inside the house.

Just like that it was over. I didn't feel sorry, just mildly disappointed that Sean hadn't turned out to be the person I thought he was.

Feeling as if I'd done the right thing, I turned around and started the long walk back to my house.

An hour later Melinda called me up. "What in the world's gotten into you? Sean told me you broke up with him. How could you do that?"

"Simple," I said. "We're not right for each other, and I told him I didn't want to see him anymore."

"How come you didn't tell me?" she asked.

"Because I knew you'd try to talk me out of it."

"Of course I would," she said. "You two had a great thing going."

"Maybe it looked that way to you. But you didn't date Sean. I did. Besides, is Sean holed up in his room crying his heart out?"

Melinda paused. "Well, no," she admitted. "But I know he cares about you."

"Look, Melinda, I like him, too. But we're not meant to be boyfriend and girlfriend. I hoped we could, but we're too different."

"But I don't remember seeing you fight."

"We didn't, but you don't have to fight to be wrong for each other," I explained. "Don't take it so hard, Melinda. Look at it this way. Now we're back to being two fun-loving girls on the loose. There's a dance this weekend, right?"

"Yeah, the annual Valentine's Day party."

"Perfect," I said. "What better time is there to start all over again?"

The dance wasn't the success I'd hoped it would be. After all, how could I be having a great time when I couldn't dance every dance?

Melinda noticed me sitting alone and came over about an hour and a half after we got there. "Why did you bother coming?" she asked bluntly.

"To have a good time, I guess," I answered.

"Do you have any idea what you look like?" She turned her face into an exaggerated frown.

I had to laugh. "Do I really look that miserable?"

She nodded. "Listen, if you're having second thoughts about Sean, I think you can still get him back. I don't think this thing with Annie's going to last."

"It's not Sean," I said. "He was right for me once, but he's not now. But I am having second thoughts."

"About Mitch?"

I nodded. "Or third or fourth thoughts—I'm not really sure. I just can't get him out of my mind, Melinda."

"I thought you said you only got along with him because you were both in the hospital."

"Maybe I was wrong. Lately I've been thinking a lot about all the wonderful things we shared. I don't think those things happened just because we were in the hospital. I think they would have happened anyway."

"Then why don't you do something about it?"

"Like what? Call him out of the blue and say, 'Hey, bud, I made a mistake. Let's party'?" I shook my head. "When he sent that picture back to me, it meant that things were over between us."

Melinda put her hands on her hips and looked at me directly. "Are you sure? If he's managed to have this kind of hold on you, then maybe he still cares about you, too."

"But what if he doesn't? I think it'd be worse having him reject me than just to wonder. At least I still have my fantasies."

"But you can't survive on fantasies forever," Melinda countered. "Isn't there some way you can get in touch with him, something that wouldn't be threatening to either of you?"

"Nothing I can think of," I said. "I can't imagine ever running into him in one of the places we hang out."

"Then maybe you need to find some new ones," she said.

I knew she was right. But I could spend the rest of my life checking out teen spots in Los Angeles trying to find him. There had to be a better way.

Chapter Fourteen

Two weeks later I saw an ad in the *Los Angeles Times* for an art show at the County Museum. Normally I wouldn't have noticed it, but this ad had "Van Gogh" in large letters across the top of it.

Mitch had mentioned once that Van Gogh was one of his favorite artists. He had to be planning on going to the show. Even so, I couldn't count on "accidentally" bumping into him there. The show was scheduled to run for weeks, and I couldn't camp out at the museum for that long.

This was one of those "nonthreatening" situations Melinda had talked about. I couldn't let the opportunity pass, so I decided to call Mitch. I could tell him about the show and hope he'd be interested in talking about more than art.

I got his number from the phone book and

began to dial. But before the call went through, I hung up. Talking over the phone was too impersonal. It would be better to stop by his house and tell him face to face. If he asked, I could always tell him I just happened to be passing by.

I skipped down the hall to my room, happy I had decided to do something instead of just worry. I opened the center drawer of my desk and pulled out the return address that I'd saved from Mitch's package.

Heading down the hall, I peeked into the spare bedroom that my mother used as an office. Mom was bent over her desk grading some papers. That was a good sign for me because it meant she planned to stay around the house for a while. "Mom," I said as I knocked on the half-opened door, "can I borrow the car?"

"Where are you going?"

"Quito Park. I've got to see a friend. I'll be back in an hour."

Mom's answer surprised me. "Absolutely not," she said, looking up from her papers.

"But why?" I demanded.

"Gretchen, you're still recovering from appendicitis. I can't let you take a chance on your driving alone. Something could happen."

I knew she was thinking about my welfare,

but I knew I could handle it. "And how long will it be before I'm recovered?" I asked. "The rest of my life? I feel fine, Mom. Really, I do."

"I still don't like the idea of your driving alone."

Then I had an idea. "What if I'm not alone?"

"I thought you said you're visiting someone."

"What if Melinda comes with me? Nothing's going to happen. But if it did, Melinda would be there to help," I added quickly.

Mom must have seen the urgency on my face because she finally gave in. "Well, all right. But don't stay long."

"Thanks, Mom." I rushed to her side and gave her a quick kiss before dashing out of the room. Then I grabbed the keys off the kitchen table and ran to the car.

Melinda was pretty surprised to see me, but she was up for the adventure. "This is the first time I've ever chaperoned a sixteen-year-old girl," she said as she slid into the seat next to me. "Where are we going, anyway?"

"To Quito Park. You can navigate for me."

"What's there? A store?"

"Is shopping all you ever think of? And, no, we're going to Mitch's house."

She smiled. "So you've decided to go for it!"

I told her about the ad. "I'll just tell him I

wanted to let him know about the show. Then I'll tell from his response whether he still feels something for me."

"So do you know where you're going? I never heard of this street."

I nodded. "I checked the map before I left. It's right off Harding Boulevard. With so little traffic, we should be able to get there in fifteen minutes."

Even after looking at the map, figuring out where I was going was tough. I'd had my license only a few months, and I still felt unsure of myself whenever I was driving in unfamiliar territory. I'd never been to Quito Park, except for a few visits to the mall there.

Pretty soon I turned onto Harding Boulevard, leaving behind the blocks of sprawling, spacious houses that made up my neighborhood. Melinda turned on the radio, filling the car with loud, bouncy music.

We passed by the Fashion Center, our favorite place to shop, and drove into an area dotted with industrial parks. I always thought industrial park was a funny name to give a business area, but in this case they did look like parks. The dark-colored, one-story buildings were beautifully landscaped with tall junipers and cedars and meticulously clipped lawns. Most of the companies made parts for computers and bore no resemblance to what most people considered factories. In fact, they blended into the scenery rather nicely.

But as we continued down the street, I began to notice subtle differences in the neighborhoods. The buildings became older, and the single-family houses slowly gave way to blocks of apartment buildings.

This area was different from my neighborhood. Instead of selling gourmet cookware, computers, video cassettes, and yoga classes, the stores here offered take-out food, shoe repair, dry cleaning, and other services for people living in apartment buildings.

"Look," Melinda said. "There's Mitch's street right there."

Off the main street the apartment buildings gave way to small but neat two-family houses. Mitch's house looked like the others in the neighborhood, and if the street number hadn't been painted on the curb, I might have passed it by completely. About the only thing that distinguished the Gantrys' green stucco house from the others was the large pot of marigolds on the brick front stoop.

So this is where Mitch lives, I thought as I looked down at the slip of paper again.

"Going in?" Melinda asked.

Taking a deep breath, I reached for the car's

door handle. "Yes," I said, my stomach a jumble of nerves. "Why would I come all this way for nothing?"

I rang the door bell several times, but nobody answered. I felt crushed. This wasn't the way it was supposed to work out.

There was nothing left for me to do but scribble my name on the ad and stuff it into the mail slot in the front door. At least he'd know I'd been there.

I returned to the car where Melinda sat tapping her hands on her knees in time to the music.

"He wasn't there," I said.

"What?" she shouted.

I turned off the radio. "Nobody's home."

Melinda sighed. "What a shame. To come all this way for nothing."

I shrugged helplessly. "Maybe it's better this way. I left the ad in the door. I know he'll get it. And if he still cares, he'll give me a call. But if he doesn't, I won't be putting him on the spot and embarrassing both of us."

"Well, then, let's get out of here," Melinda said. "We've got a phone call to wait for."

"Don't worry, I'm going," I said as I put my key in the ignition.

But he didn't call.

Melinda waited with me in my room till her mother called her to come home for dinner. "Keep your spirits up," she told me. "He probably hasn't come home yet."

"Yes," I agreed. "He told me he had a part-time job before he got hurt. Maybe he's gone back to it."

That excuse seemed reasonable enough at the time, but as the hours stretched into night time, it began to wear thin. Of course, there could have been some other explanation for why he didn't call back that night—maybe some special event at school or a project at a friend's house.

But as the days went by and he didn't call, there was only one explanation that made sense. He just didn't care about me anymore.

Chapter Fifteen

The following Tuesday I stood in front of the mirror checking out how I looked in my cheerleader's uniform. The red jumper fit just fine, and it felt great to have it on. Just the day before, Dr. Benard had given me the OK to rejoin the squad, and I was getting ready for the basketball game that night against Southgate High. Even though I was out of practice, I felt strong enough to keep up with the rest of the squad.

During the past couple of weeks I'd been getting up early each morning and working out a little. I'd started with walks around the block, and I was up to jogging half a mile. It was important for me to get back into shape as quickly as I could. Track season was coming up soon, and I was hoping I'd be able to make the team again. There was no way I would unless I started working at it right away.

Not wanting to look like a complete fool at the game that night, I fished my red and white pompoms out of my closet and began to run through some cheers. "B-E-A-T-E-M! B-E-A-T-E-M. Beat 'em! Beat 'em, boys. Beat 'em!" I cried, waving my pompoms in the air. It felt good to do that again. I started another. "The Warriors are on the warpath tonight. We're going to show you all our might. Go, Warriors! Fight! Fight! Fight!"

A satisfying feeling rushed through me. It was the same kind of high you get from saying the right thing at the right time or getting an A on a test or saying no to an ice-cream sundae when you're on a diet.

The sound of a car horn interrupted my thoughts. Lindsay had come to pick me up. I was ready to make my comeback appearance.

It was a home game, and after the guys were through with their pregame practice, I took my spot on the court with the rest of the squad. We did the usual pump-up-the-crowd stuff—a couple of walking cheers, a few somersaults, and finally our human pyramid. That one was a little rough for me since I was on the bottom row and had all that weight to support. But fortunately it was over soon, and I took a seat on the front row bleacher reserved for us. I was grateful for the short rest we'd get before the team was introduced.

It felt a little funny, cheering enthusiastically when Sean's name was called. In the time since we'd broken up, we'd barely spoken to each other. I wasn't brokenhearted about it; I knew I had done the right thing. Still, I couldn't help looking at him wistfully, wishing that things could have worked out differently.

I felt the same way as I scanned the bleachers on the other side of the court.

"Looking for anyone special?" Lindsay asked.

Melinda, sitting in the row right above us, spoke up. "Of course she is. Southgate is Mitch's school."

I didn't want to make a big deal out of it. Since he hadn't called or anything, I'd tried to play down my interest in Mitch to my friends. But that didn't mean that I'd stopped caring or that I wasn't hoping he'd be there—just that I didn't want to publicize my feelings.

I stretched my arms in and out, waving my pompoms in little circles, pretending to be more interested in perfecting my cheers than talking about Mitch.

"Yes, it's his school," I said, "but that

doesn't necessarily mean he's here. In fact, he probably isn't. He's an artist, you know, and artists usually aren't into sports."

Melinda wasn't buying my rationale. "All the kids at Southgate are artists. If your theory were true, they wouldn't be able to field a basketball team that may be in the championships, let alone have anyone interested in seeing their games. And as you can see"—she pointed to the other side of the court—"there are quite a few Southgate fans here."

I looked over. The seats reserved for the opposing team were almost filled. A bunch of kids had even brought along signs saying stuff like, "Go, Southgate" and "Conquer Those Warriors." But I couldn't get a good enough look at the crowd to tell if Mitch was there.

I willed myself to concentrate on the game. The Brimley Warriors were in first place in the conference, with Southgate just one game behind. That night's game was an important one. I held my breath when our center, Bobby Maron, and the center from Southgate faced each other for the opening jump.

Fortunately Bobby got it and threw the ball downcourt to Sean, who passed it to Ron Knox. Ron made a nifty move around one of the Southgate guys to stuff the ball into the hoop.

We were off to a good start, and I couldn't help feeling that things were going to go our way that evening.

At the end of the first quarter, we were four points behind, but during the second quarter we evened up the score. Being at home had to be making the difference. Between our squad's shouts and the cheers from the crowd, we were making Southgate feel they were in very hostile territory.

Then it happened. There was only about a minute left before halftime. Along with the other cheerleaders I was pumping up the Brimley crowd even more, making sure that when the guys went into the locker room they'd know we were really rooting for them. After finishing the cheer, I waved my pompoms in the air. Just as I turned around to watch the action on the court, I thought I saw Mitch in the opposite bleachers. He was making his way to the aisle, his face partially turned to the side so I couldn't get a really good look at him. But he had wavy, dark hair. It had to be Mitch.

A strange feeling came over me. It was sort of like the adrenaline rush I got just before a race. I felt nervous, anxious, and more than a little excited. *He's here! He's really here!* I kept telling myself.

He looked as if he were headed toward the concession stand just outside the gymnasium. I toyed briefly with the idea of sneaking out right then and there, but we were supposed to stay in the gym until the buzzer. I looked up at the clock. *Thirty-two seconds. Well, that's not too bad,* I told myself. *He can't go too far in half a minute.*

But three seconds later Sean was fouled by one of the Southgate forwards. Sean was one of those players who loved standing at the foul line. His hands on his hips, he looked insulted while he waited for the referee to announce the infraction. When he heard the call, "Defensive foul on number twenty-three, Flanders, by number thirty-one, Winston," he perked up, loving having everyone's eyes on him.

He milked the incident for all it was worth. As soon as he got the ball, he dribbled it for what seemed like ages before positioning it for the first throw. Then he stared at the hoop, mentally completing the toss before he threw the ball.

He missed, but he had two shots coming so he went through the whole process again. He missed again and was saved from humiliation only because Jeremy grabbed the rebound and stuffed it into the basket. But all this had taken more than three minutes in real time, and there were still twenty-seven seconds on the clock. At that rate I'd never get to see Mitch.

As soon as the buzzer sounded, I bolted from the bleachers and headed for the concession stand. I was hoping that Mitch had been thirsty or hungry and gone there during the break in the action. Out of curiosity Lindsay had followed me, but this was one time I didn't want her company. Fortunately, I spotted Melinda and Betsy walking out and steered Lindsay in their direction.

But Melinda saw me, too, and had to run over. "Gretchen, how are you making out?"

I couldn't leave them. "I'm still in one piece. Really, I'm feeling fine," I said, groaning inwardly.

"What a game," Betsy said. "I think our guys are going to kill them."

"No thanks to Sean," Melinda scoffed. "Can you believe the way he's shooting? You'd think he never held a basketball in his life!"

"Hey, don't be so hard on him," Lindsay put in. "Jeremy's taking up the slack."

"Sure, you'd notice that," Melinda said.

"Well, he *is* my boyfriend."

While they were talking, I took the opportunity to slink away toward the popcorn vendor. That dark, wavy-haired head was still visible, but the crowd around him was growing as people exited the gym. Squeezing my way through the pack, I got to within an arm's length of him.

Realizing that he might not be able to hear me in the clamor of voices surrounding us, I reached out and tapped him on the back.

The boy who turned around wasn't Mitch! He looked puzzled, which wasn't surprising since he'd probably never seen me before in his life. "Uh, excuse me," I finally managed to say. "I thought you were someone else."

He smiled and turned back to the counter. I, meanwhile, headed toward the ladies' room, definitely in need of a few minutes to recover. I splashed water on my face, trying to cool off the flush of embarrassment that had come over me. I felt absolutely miserable. It wasn't just the shock of having bothered a stranger or even the feeling that I'd made a fool out of myself. It was the realization that I'd been building up my hopes for something I knew would never happen.

It was stupid to have believed Mitch would be at the game. Surely he had better things to do with his life. Despite what Melinda said, I was willing to bet that at that moment Mitch was out with his friends. Doing what, I didn't know. We lived totally different lives. It was just fate that had brought us together for those days in the hospital, and I had to accept that before I allowed it to drive me crazy.

I left the bathroom just in time to join the others back on the court for our halftime routine. I was grateful that I had the cheers to keep me busy. At least they'd keep my mind off my misery.

Still, I couldn't wait till the game was over and I could go home. But the second half seemed to drag on forever. Every time our team started to pull ahead, the Southgate guys would foul Sean. All they managed to do was slow down the game. Having been embarrassed by his first-half performance, Sean recovered his shooting ability and sank every foul shot he tried.

Mercifully the game finally ended. Even though Brimley won, I didn't feel much like cheering. I trailed behind Lindsay and Melinda as they walked happily out of the gym.

We caught up with Betsy, Clare, and Amy outside near the parking lot. Already the cool night was alive with beeping car horns proclaiming Brimley's victory. I felt hands patting me on the back in congratulations as if our cheering had had something to do with the win.

"Say, where do you guys want to go to celebrate?" Melinda cried out. "The Cat?"

"Naw, it'll be too crowded," Betsy complained.

"That's exactly why we should go there," Melinda replied. "I'd love to be surrounded by a horde of happy Brimley guys. What do you say, Gretch?" She looked at me.

I shrugged. "I don't know. I'm feeling tired. I think I'll go home and make it an early night."

"Party pooper." Clare frowned. "I'm with Melinda. I want to go where the boys are."

"Speaking of boys, Gretchen," Betsy interjected, "isn't that Mitch over there by the water fountain?"

I couldn't bear to turn around. I stood stock-still, frozen by fear and indecision. I'd spent the past hour and a half trying to tell myself I didn't want to see him again. Now what? What would I say to him? What *could* I say?

I turned around and walked slowly toward the water fountain near the back door of the gym. Lots of cheering kids were still pouring out the door toward me, and it was almost like swimming upstream. But I didn't care. It didn't matter what I'd just told myself; I still cared for Mitch very much. Just because he was here was no guarantee that he still felt the same way about me, but at least I'd be able to find out once and for all.

I caught his eye. He looked as good as I'd remembered. Better, actually, since he was wearing a royal blue sweater and a pair of tight-fitting jeans that showed off his lean body.

As I drew closer, the sparkle in his eyes seemed to grow brighter. He managed a little smile. "Hi, Gretchen," he said softly.

I wanted to put my arms around him so badly, but I held back, afraid of what his reaction would be. "Hi, Mitch." I smiled back. "Hey, you got your cast off."

"Yesterday." He showed me his arm. "It couldn't stay on forever. I healed quicker than they expected. It's just like the doctor promised—good as new."

"That's great."

"I see you're doing better, too." He pointed to the pompoms I still held in my hands. "I didn't expect to see you leading cheers. The last time I saw you, you could hardly stand up."

"Was I really that bad?" I asked.

He grinned. "I don't think you really want me to answer that."

"You're right. I don't." I took a deep breath. "How's it going?"

"Fine. I'm back at my gardening job. Just mowing, though. I'm not ready to tackle any chain saws yet."

"I got the sketch you sent me. Thanks."

"I remembered how disappointed you were when I wouldn't give it to you in the hospital. I thought you'd really like to have it now."

"So have you done any more?"

He nodded. "A few. After doing yours I decided to sketch some of the other hospital patients I visit."

"But I thought you didn't go to the hospital anymore!" I blurted out.

He didn't ask me how I knew. "I thought I told you I do volunteer work at Quito Park General."

"I thought you meant Brimley."

"No, I just ended up there because it was closer to where I had my accident. Quito's not too far from my house."

"I see."

"How about you?" he asked. "What have you been doing?"

"Oh, nothing much, really," I said. "School, running in the mornings. Sounds kind of boring, doesn't it?"

"Not at all. How's your genetics report?"

"I finished it last week. I'm really pleased with it. I should be, considering all the work I put into it."

If my conversation was less than sparkling, it had nothing at all to do with the way I was feeling. No, I take that back. It had *everything* to do with it. I was afraid to turn the talk to us, to talk about anything personal. I also kept thinking about the art show ad and that Mitch hadn't responded to it. Maybe he was just talking to me now for old times' sake. Maybe he'd come to the game because he really was a basketball fan, and it had just been chance that we happened to meet again.

All I knew was that I didn't have the nerve to bring it up.

But apparently Mitch did. "And how's Sean?" he asked. "Uh, you don't have to tell me about his basketball ability. I've seen that."

"We broke up, this time for good," I said simply.

"You did?" Mitch said, giving me the strangest look, a cross between shock, dread, and pleasure. I had no idea what the look meant.

Mitch looked at me seriously. "We've got to talk, Gretchen."

Chapter Sixteen

"OK, let's talk," I said.

"It's too noisy here. Come with me," he said.

"Where're we going?"

Mitch smiled mysteriously. "You'll see."

Taking my hand he led me through the crowd to the parking lot, where lots of kids were laughing and shouting. We had to dart to the curb at one point to avoid a car with a boy hanging out the passenger door shouting, "We're number one! We're number one!" In my haste to get out of the way, I stumbled on a piece of gravel and nearly fell, but Mitch steadied me.

"Thanks," I said gratefully.

Mitch smiled as if it were nothing, but as we walked I saw him rubbing the arm he'd grabbed me with. Then I realized it was the one he'd broken. "Oh, Mitch, I'm so sorry," I said. "Does your arm hurt?"

"It's all right," he said. Then in a very soft voice, I thought I heard him mumble, "I think everything's going to be all right now."

I didn't want to press the issue right then, but it looked like a good sign. Steadying myself, I followed Mitch to a small white Chevy.

We rode past the Cheshire Cat, then turned down Harding Boulevard. Mitch was quiet at first, looking straight ahead at the traffic and rapping his fingers against the steering wheel as if he were trying to think of the right words to say.

I was terrified he'd spend the whole ride in silence, so I found the courage to say at least part of what was on my mind. "I'm really glad to see you. I've missed you a lot, Mitch."

He smiled and turned to me as if he were going to say something, but then turned to face the road again.

I gulped. What was going on? Wasn't he glad to see me? Why was he taking me for a ride if he wasn't? "Listen, Mitch, I know I hurt you the last time we were together, and you have every right to hate me. But don't play games with me. If you don't want to have anything to do with me, then take me home right now."

He continued driving, but a few moments

later he spoke up. "You and Sean really broke up?"

"About three weeks ago."

"Why?"

"We don't really have anything in common. I think deep down I've known it all along, but I used to gloss over our differences as if they didn't matter. It was only after I got out of the hospital that a lot of the stuff I used to tolerate about him started to bother me."

"What about the history you two had?"

"I realized that I needed more than that."

Mitch pulled into a parking lot. "Well, here we are," he said, turning off the ignition.

I glanced up at the sign. "Tito's?"

Mitch smiled shyly. "I thought you might be in the mood to celebrate. I know you love the food here."

"I don't care about the basketball game."

"I don't either. I wasn't talking about basketball; I was talking about us."

Did he say what I thought he'd said? "Us?"

He nodded. "As in you and I. Together." Leaning over the center console, he held my face in his hands and placed his lips on mine. The kiss was as sweet as any I could remember. "I've missed you so much, Gretchen."

I answered by sliding closer and giving him the biggest hug I'd ever given anyone. "I'm so glad to hear you say that. I never thought I would."

We went inside, snuggling together in one of the booths. I ordered a chili burrito, but I was so jumpy inside I didn't think I'd be able to eat it. The last thing on my mind at that moment was food.

For a long time we just sat there, holding hands and saying nothing. That was the great thing about Mitch. Just being with him was enough. I didn't feel the need to try to impress him, and he didn't demand it of me. He'd seen me at my worst and had been able to discover something about me that he found special. It didn't matter that we went to different schools. It didn't matter that he was into art and I was into science. What was important was that we enjoyed each other—even though it had taken me a little longer to find that out than it did him.

After our food came, I decided to tell him. "When you sent that sketch of me back, I was afraid it meant you never wanted to see me again."

He nodded. "When I left Melinda's party, I didn't think I would. I knew I couldn't take just being your friend."

"Is that why you didn't call after I left the ad in your door?" I wondered.

"I wasn't really sure what to make of that. I thought it was your way of trying to be nice, but I wasn't ready to let go of my dream of us together. I started to call you several times, but I was afraid of listening to your latest date with Sean. I wanted to see you so badly that finally I decided to give myself this one last shot by coming to the game. I figured if you said you were still with Sean, that'd be it. But I had to hear it from you in person."

"Sean and I are definitely history—past history," I said.

He squeezed my hand tightly. "That's really good news, because I have something to show you." He pulled out an envelope from his back pocket.

"What's that?"

"Two tickets to the art show at the county museum. I plan to take someone special."

"Do I know her?" I asked.

"I think I'm looking right at her."

"It's a date," I said.

"Not yet."

"What do you mean?"

"We have to seal it with a kiss."

Dropping the envelope on the table, Mitch pulled me into his arms and kissed me. "That one was for the art show," he said. "And these are for all the dates yet to come."

We hope you enjoyed reading this book. All the titles currently available in the Sweet Dreams series are listed on page two. They are all available at your local bookshop or newsagent, though should you find any difficulty in obtaining the books you would like, you can order direct from the publisher, at the address below. Also, if you would like to know more about the series, or would simply like to tell us what you think of the series, write to:

Kim Prior,
Sweet Dreams,
Transworld Publishers Limited,
61–63 Uxbridge Road,
Ealing, London W5 5SA.

To order books, please list the title(s) you would like, and send together with your name and address, and a cheque or postal order made payable to TRANSWORLD PUBLISHERS LIMITED. Please allow cost of book(s) plus 20p for the first book and 10p for each additional book for postage and packing.

(The above applies to readers in the UK and Ireland only.)

If you live in Australia or New Zealand, and would like more information about the series, please write to:

Sally Porter,
Sweet Dreams
Corgi & Bantam Books,
26 Harley Crescent,
Condell Park,
N.S.W. 2200,
Australia.

Kiri Martin
Sweet Dreams
c/o Corgi & Bantam Books
New Zealand,
Cnr. Moselle and Waipareira
Avenues,
Henderson,
Auckland,
New Zealand.